Laurie Graham is a former *Daily Telegraph* columnist and contributing editor of *She* magazine. She is the author of several acclaimed novels, the most recent being *At Sea*. Laurie lives in Dublin. Visit her website at www.lauriegraham.com

'A joy to read. It's funny and passionate and encapsulates an era of wistful innocence.' Maureen Lipman

'What a wonderful, life-unhancing, truly funny writer she is.' Elizabeth Buchanan

'Laurie Graham, what a find! I was only about three sentences into *At Sea* when I knew I was going to savour every sentence and bitterly mourn the end . . . The kind of book you stay awake far later than you should do reading, only to wake bleary eyed the next day thinking of the time when you can pick it up again.'
Wendy Holden

'She has wit and insight to match Nick Hornby, and the entertainment vale of Helen Fielding, as well as dep   *ndependent*

Also by Laurie Graham

The Man for the Job
The Ten O'Clock Horses
Perfect Meringues
The Dress Circle
The Future Homemakers of America
The Unfortunates
Mr. Starlight
Gone With the Windsors
The Importance of Being Kennedy
Life According to Lubka
At Sea

Dog Days, Glenn Miller Nights

Laurie Graham

Quercus

First published in Great Britain in 2000 by Black Swan
This paperback edition published in 2011 by

Quercus
55 Baker Street
7th Floor, South Block
London
W1U 8EW

A CIP catalogue record for this book is available
from the British Library

ISBN 978 1 84916 398 9

10 9 8 7 6 5 4 3 2 1

Typeset by Ellipsis Digital Limited, Glasgow

Printed and bound in Great Britain by Clays Ltd, St Ives plc

For Hilda
and for all the girls who made the thing that
drilled the hole that held the spring . . .

I'd just come out onto the walkway to see if there was a signal from Clarice. From Apple Bough you can look straight across to Cherry Tree, so that's the arrangement. Twice a day: in the morning to see her curtains are open, which means she hasn't passed over in the night, and then later on to see if her big plaster swan is on her window sill, which is her way of letting me know the helper has been and got her washed and dressed, otherwise she'd still be sitting there in her nightie come teatime. That's how you have to carry on when you're old.

I go in to see Clarice every day, after I've fetched her a few bits from the Wavy Line, and she gives me her list for the next day. Helpers aren't supposed to do shopping, nor housework. It's because of the cutbacks. Why they're called helpers beats me.

Life'd be a lot easier if Clarice would get the phone

1

put in, but she won't because she's worried about running up bills and finishing up in the workhouse. Somebody said to me that the social would probably pay some of it for her, with her being housebound, but I don't know if it's even worth asking. They'll be the same kind of dimwits that put her on the fifth floor, with everybody talking Punjabi. She should get something paid for, by rights, because she's not out causing wear and tear on the pavements, or tripping up on broken flagstones and claiming compensation. And she's not used the street lighting in years. All that ought to count for something, but you can bet your sweet life there'd be something in the small print. Money in the bank, for one thing. If you've worked hard all your life and put a bit by, they won't give you a brass farthing.

And yet I read in my paper how there's all this money lying there unclaimed. Millions lying around because people don't know they're entitled. Not round here, though. Round here they could sign claim forms for England. So I came out onto the walkway, and there was Snake Eye in the corner, answering a call of nature. I said, 'You idle hound. You only need to walk ten steps and you could do that in your mother's toilet.' He just gave me the finger. Bloody kids. Twenty-six and he's still piddling in the passageways.

Anyway, I spotted that reverend with the bad teeth just coming out of Clarice's, so I knew she was all right. He takes her a little magazine once a month and sits with her for half an hour. He knocked my door once trying to get me to go to some women's thing, Tuesday afternoons. Bible stories and tea from an urn. I told him I'd never been a pew-kisser and he said, 'That's all right. You're still very welcome.' But I still wouldn't have his magazine. He's only Church of England, but give any of those padres an inch and they'll take the full mile.

Young Clark was hanging about on the landing.

He said, 'Hello, Mrs Gibbs. The lift's not working again.'

I said, 'Why aren't you in school?'

'Baker Day,' he said.

No wonder they're still having reading lessons when they're sixteen. They are always out doing projects, hanging round the precinct with clipboards, or going on trips. And then they get these Baker Days, and they're roaming round here, drinking Thunderbird and up to no good. Clark's all right. Looks like a skinned rabbit, but he's a kind-hearted boy. Always gives me a hand if I've got a heavy bag. But the rest of them; they'd knock your lights out as soon as look at you.

Clark said, 'Mrs Rankin's won a car.' And there she was, down on the fifth with Clark's nan, yoo-hooing me.

'Birdie,' she goes, 'I've had a bit of luck. I definitely might have won a car.' Always doing competitions, Olive. And scratch cards and bingo. She never wins anything. Clarice does crosswords, and one time she did win a fancy fountain pen, worth pounds, although why anybody would bother I don't know, when you can get a biro in Kareem's Kabin for ten pence and chuck it out when it's finished. You don't want valuables when you get to our time of life. You want a pair of knees that don't hurt.

She said, 'It's just come – second post. All I have to do is order something from this catalogue and then my name goes up for the car. Course, I'd have to get someone to fetch it for me. I wouldn't know which pedal is which. Brian'll fetch it.' Brian's her lad. He lives in Wanstead Park with his lady friend, and he's not worked in years. Did his back in, lifting boxes at the parcel depot, and he's never worked since. They've all got bad backs round here. You'd think it was catching.

I said, 'Have they got anything you want in the catalogue?'

'I'll find something,' she said, and Blanche said, 'I might have a look in it myself.' Blanche is Clark's nan. She's had him since he was a little baby, so he's never known any different.

Everybody tells a different story about Clark's mum: she's in Australia, last heard of with some big ugly biker; she's in one of those hospitals with her hair cut short. As a matter of fact, I think she's probably on the game somewhere. But Blanche never says a word. Clark thinks she's in heaven. It's his dad he's always moithering about. He asked me once if I thought Snake Eye might be his dad.

I said, 'I hope not, Superman. You deserve a lot better than that.'

He said, 'Yeah. My real dad'll be coming to get me, some day.'

Clarice wanted a tin of Tip-Top, a small white sliced and the *Herald*, because they were giving a free Spontex with every copy.

I said, 'I see you had a visitor this morning.'

She said, 'Three visitors, Birdie. Three in one day. Four if I count you, which I do. So aren't I the lucky one?'

Apart from the reverend, she'd had Wilf Orme rapping her window, looking for me, and a Mr Swift from Aldersbrook Comprehensive offering to get her bedroom painted for her. Wilf must have just missed me. He knows my routine.

She said, 'I told the man my bedroom doesn't really need doing, but he said it's for Community Awareness Week. He said it wouldn't cost me anything. What do you think?'

I said, 'What? Kids from Aldersbrook, out painting

houses? I wouldn't let them through the door.'

They want to get teaching them to add up, never mind about community awareness. They want to teach them how to spell. Clarice is too trusting.

I said, 'They'll be rifling through your drawers, looking for your bank book.'

She said, 'Oh dear. Perhaps I'll tell him no thank you. Let somebody else have my turn.'

Wilf was round the back of Almond Blossom picking up rubbish. Fag packets and beer cans and burger boxes. He said, 'Look at this.' He'd found two French letters and one of those disposable nappies. Every day he's down there with his dustbin liner. He says, 'You have to keep trying, Birdie. You can't give in to it.' He's the same with his allotment. There's dogs get onto it and kids trampling everything down, and he's never done much good with carrots. They come out all top and no bottom. But he's still down there in all weathers. And he brings me lettuces and sprouting broc and beetroot, and nine times out of ten it goes in the bin, because I can't be bothered with all that any more. Not since I got my microwave. If I could have had the pill and my microwave in 1946 I'd have been a very happy woman.

I walked back with him as far as Orange Grove, but I didn't go in. He's been after me for years to hand in my rent book and get hitched, but it doesn't appeal to me. Sitting there, night after night, him leafing through his gardening books and me having to keep the sound down on the telly. And he never plays records. All he listens to is gardening talks on the wireless. If he wasn't so quiet I might have considered it, because he has kept himself nice. It's seventeen years since he lost his Evelyn, but he's always put his best foot forward. Always wears a tie, even on the allotment. And he's handy; he makes cakes and Christmas puddings. You do miss a body to warm your feet on, but you get used to it, and I'm up till all hours with Glenn Miller. Besides, what would we do with two sideboards?

Those girls were loafing around outside his tower. Great ugly lumps in their big, black puffed-up jackets and their great clodhopping feet. People used to have to wear boots like that if they'd had polio, and you felt sorry for them.

Wilf said, 'Hello, Gemma. You want to cut out those cigarettes. They'll stunt your growth.'

If only. I don't know how he remembers which one's which. They all look the same to me: Gemma, Shannon, Jodie, Nikki, Tamsin. There's hardly a one of them got a normal name. There was a Samantha as well, always tagged along with them, but she's got a little brown baby now, so she hangs about with a different crowd. Still puffing on her fags, though. Still effing and jeffing and wearing her polio shoes.

He said, 'I suppose I can't tempt you to a nice pot of tea and a custard tart?', but I'm not a big tea-drinker these days, and I wanted to get back. It looked as though Raelene was getting some bad news over the phone at the end of the last episode, just as all the names and the music started rolling, and I wanted to see if it was a death or just a coma. They haven't had a coma for a long while.

I like to shut my door, get my shoes off and have a glass of stout with my choccie bar. Then I'm ready for my programmes. There are plenty of good things about being a poor old soul and living all on your ownsome. You don't have to peel spuds for anybody's tea, or ask them if they mind you changing channels. If I want a bit of company there's always Olive or Blanche, although lately they're bingo crazy. Three nights a week they go, four sometimes, if there's a cash rollover or a prize they're after, like a Christmas hamper. I'd sooner watch paint dry.

A nice little dance hall is what I'd like to go to. The Imperial used to be my favourite, but the Sikhs have got it now for a temple, and anyway, you can't get the men. Herbie Ford used to be a lovely mover, but his wife's an invalid. Fine-looking girl she was, with red curly hair, and now they've had to have a hoist put in and everything, so I don't suppose he's ever going to feel like dancing again.

I had a Pot Mash and another stout, and I was just settling down to watch *University Challenge* when there was a right racket started outside, banging and screaming and shouting. I tried to see from the kitchen window, because you have to be careful, going outside at night. You never know what you're going to find. I thought it might be one of Patti's husbands come back, full of ale and looking for money, but the noise was coming from Dawn and Snake Eye's side. And that really could mean trouble.

Now if Clarice had done like I said and got herself a phone, I could have called her up and said, 'Take a look out of your window and tell me if I've got police on my walkway.' I tried Olive, but there was no answer, so I tried Blanche. I got Clark.

He said, 'Nan's at bingo.'

I said, 'Can you see if there's a police van down below?'

He was gone a minute or two.

'Can't see anything,' he said. 'Did you send for them?'

I told him about the shenanigans outside. He said, 'Don't worry, Mrs Gibbs. I'll come up.'

I said, 'Don't you dare. You stay put till your nan gets back.'

We used to go everywhere in the blackout and never think anything of it, and now it isn't even safe to put your nose out of your door. And Clark shouldn't even be left, not till he's fourteen or something. Somebody told Blanche that and she was worried they might send somebody round and put him in care, so she cut back on her bingo for a week or two, but as Olive said, when we were Clark's age we were damned near ready to leave school. We'd got Hitler shaping up to bomb the living daylights out of us. I know they have to stay on till they're sixteen now, and Clark does look a lot younger than he acts, but there are plenty round here not much older than him, pushing prams. I can't make any sense of it.

Anyway, next thing was, Dawn was hammering on my door.

'Help me, Birdie,' she was calling. I couldn't leave her out there. So I let her in and put the chain back on, fast as I could.

She said they'd got the wrong flat. She said they'd got him mixed up with some other bad lot, but they hadn't. He's trouble. She didn't want me to call the law. Begged me not to. But I'm not having men coming onto my walkway with baseball bats threatening to cave people's heads in. Not even Snake Eye's head. She says he's never given her any worry, but that's silly mother talk. She says he's got a learning disability, and he gets discrimination down the Job Centre because he's off-white, but I doubt they've ever seen him at any Job Centre. She reckons he's trying to get a little business going. Got his name down for a stall in Queen's Market, and he's doing a bit of buying and selling at home till the paperwork comes through.

I don't think so. I suppose there might come a day when you can go down the market to buy the stuff he sells, but they'll have screwed the lid down on my box by then, I hope. His too, the way he carries on.

The lifts were still out, so the boys in blue needed oxygen by the time they'd run up all those stairs. It's no wonder Olive needs new hips.

It turned out Snake Eye had had a visit from the Grievers. They're an outfit from the Clover Farm Estate, and Dwayne, who's the big man Snake Eye runs errands for, has been messing with their big man, or some such story. Who cares? They're called the Grievers, as in Grievers Bodily Harm, so they're not just evil, they're morons as well.

Anyway, they'd booted Dawn's bedroom door down because Snake Eye had shut himself in there, and they'd ruined a chest of drawers she hadn't even finished paying for, but Snake Eye had got out across the balconies and scarpered. She swore she didn't know any names, but she promised she'd go down the station and have a look at some faces. I made the lads a quick Nescaff. Chasing up all those stairs, and her not even willing to make a complaint. PC Smalley is supposed to be our neighbourhood bobby, and he's got a new partner, PC Lines. Neither of them looks a day over twenty, and yet Ian Smalley's got a wife and two tiny tots at home – little girls. He showed me a photo once.

The new one said, 'Will you be all right, Gran?' I told him, I'm not anybody's gran, and Dawn said, 'Never mind about her. I'm the one with a ruined door.' So the next time she comes crying for help, I shall just turn the telly up louder. And I missed my quiz.

Blanche phoned me when she got in. She said, 'I hear you've had a bit of excitement.'

I said, 'I don't call it excitement, living next door to hooligans. Getting out once in a while would be excitement. Seeing the outside of these four walls after dark.'

'Well,' she said, 'you know you're always welcome to come to bingo.'

I said, 'And I don't call that excitement either, sitting holding a magic marker, waiting for that rug-head to shout out numbers.' It's a well-known fact Dickie Smart hasn't got a natural hair on his head due to alopecia. I said, 'There's no skill in it, Blanche. It's not poker. Sitting with a bunch of daft women.'

She said, 'We get men.'

Not the kind of men I'm interested in. You get the ones that are handcuffed to their wives, that's all. Why else would they be there? Bingo's not a natural activity for a man.

'Oh well,' she said, 'I can see there's no pleasing you tonight. I only phoned because Clark was worried you'd been murdered.' And she put the phone down on me. So I'm in her bad books, and if I'm in hers I'll be in Olive's, because they're joined at the neck lately, those two. Sometimes I think I should just go away somewhere. By the sea would be nice, somewhere they have tea dances. You do hear of people swapping flats, but who'd want to swap a place at the seaside for this midden? They called it slum clearance when they put us in here, but I think we were better off ten to a toilet down Hope Street.

I watched the news. The Queen Mother's in hospital. They say there's no cause for concern, but the papers are all waiting outside, up their step-ladders with their cameras. And vans pulling up all the time, delivering flowers. It must be like Kew Gardens in there, unless they pass some of them on, straight out the back door to the underprivileged. I tell you. You wouldn't want to be in the same hospital as royalty if you were troubled by pollen.

I met her once. December 1944, when she reviewed us at Lambeth. She was Queen then, of course. She had Princess Elizabeth with her, and she came along the line and said we'd done a wonderful job. God, it was a cold day, and my chilblains were giving me gyp, but the newsreel people were there, and I got a free ticket to see the rushes at the Leicester Square Rialto. I've had excitement in my life. Not lately though.

I went up West for the day. Had a cream slice in Peter Jones, stocked up on my Clairol and went to a matinée at the Victoria Palace – *Sweet Charity*. Olive says she doesn't know how I do it, but it's not bad if you go after the rush and use your pensioner's pass. And I don't waste money on dinners like she does. Roasted Chicken Platter, Hake in Breadcrumbs, Faggots in Gravy. It's like Tesco's inside her fridge. I couldn't be bothered with all that, sitting at a table on your own, and then washing up. Couple of those little Twix bars and I'm happy.

I was just coming out of Upton Park tube and I heard someone say, 'Gibbs? Is that you?' and I smelled the Brylcreem. Jimmy Dwyer, in a shortie mac and a pair of those running shoes. He'd lost his teeth and most of his hair, but nothing else much had changed. Still held his cigarette between his thumb and his finger.

I said, 'How did you spot me?' I don't even recognize myself these days. They've got a telly screen in the Wavy Line these days, because of all the thieving, and I looked up at it one time and I thought, Who's that little old dear?

He said, 'I'd know them legs anywhere.'

He'd got a dog with him, lovely brindle and white with a nice head.

I said, 'You're not still in the business?'

'No,' he said. 'I'm just minding her. She broke her wrist and they never got her fit after that, never raced her again. This bloke I know took her in, and when he has to go away, I mind her. She's nice company. You on your own, Birdie?'

I met Jimmy Dwyer in '42, when they sent me down to Saltdean. He was a kennel lad at Brighton, failed his call-up medical because of bad feet, and he was put on fire-watch at the stadium, because if ever they'd got bombed he'd have known what to do with the dogs. I liked being at the seaside, but there was nothing much happening. It was like there wasn't even a war on, after the drubbing we'd had in London.

Me and a girl called Pearl were down there together, and we got a bit of work assembling aircraft parts. Pearl was a laugh. We got into the area agility team, because we were both light enough to stand on a man's shoulders, but then she took the elastic out of the legs of her drawers and put a bit of lace on them, said it was part of her war effort, and she got charged with damaging government property. And we had a station officer – prune-faced old misery, never satisfied with anything – and he told Pearl she made the worst cup of tea he'd ever tasted, so the next brew she made for him he got a good helping of Epsom salts in it. I had some great times with Pearl. She didn't make it through to the end, though. Only twenty-two. I often think of her.

Anyway, I quite liked the dogs and Jimmy quite liked me, so that was how it started, and you had your fun while you could in those days. He had his looks then and so did I.

I said, 'What bloke? Where are you staying?'

'Down towards East Ham,' he said. 'He's gone to Tenerife and you can't take dogs. Where are you nowadays, Birdie?'

I told him about Apple Bough. Living up that high it makes your head spin, and nowhere to hang your washing. Chains on your door and eyes in the back of your head if you set foot outside. We've had muggings and robbings. Some poor Paki family, minding their own business, got burned out of their flat, and Olive had her transistor thieved off her kitchen window sill, and she was only sitting in the next room. Almond Blossom's the worst. They've had shootings over there.

'Give up your own place, did you?' he said, fishing. I never had a place to give up. Always rented. Always thought I'd get a proper place later on, if things worked out. Next thing you know you're fifty-nine and they're having a whip-round to buy you a retirement clock.

He said, 'I shall have to come round and see you. Take you out for a few drinks. Talk about the old days.'

He got me to write it all down on an old betting slip. He said, 'How are you fixed tomorrow?'

I said, 'I won't hold my breath.'

'No,' he said. 'If I say I'll come tomorrow, I'll come tomorrow. And I'll bring Vanessa. She's taken a shine to you.'

Her racing name was Pepper Pot. He never did tell me where he was staying.

Blanche was on my doorstep first thing. She'd brought me Clarice's shopping list and she wanted to tell me the chemist's might be closing down, in the precinct. There's a story going round it's going to be another video shop, so somebody's getting up a petition. Then if Kareem goes, which he keeps threatening to do if he has his windows broken many more times, we won't even have a post office. It'll mean a bus ride for everything. You'll have to spend your pension fetching your pension. And your tablets. All we'll have left soon is a chipper, an off-licence and a place to get videos. Rubbish for the belly and rubbish for the mind, that's what Wilf says. And it's nearly as bad off the estate. It's all card shops and scented candles, and Multimedia, whatever that is when it's at home.

Blanche said, 'Clark went across with her ham and her newspaper yesterday, when he got in from school, but he said she wouldn't open the door properly. Kept it on the chain, and he had to pass the stuff to her through the gap. She kept saying she'd never asked for any painting to be done. He told her who he was, but it didn't make any difference. I was going to go across myself, make sure she was all right, but Olive said it'd be best not to confuse her any more, best leave well alone till you got back. You'd think they'd get her into a place with a warden, really, if her mind's starting to go.'

It's not Clarice's mind that's going. It's her insides.

I said to Blanche, 'Not letting some boy in you don't even recognize, that's a good sign. That means the wick's definitely still dipping in the oil. She wouldn't remember Clark. When does she ever see him? She did the right thing not letting him in. I should have thought you could have gone yourself and sat with her for five minutes. Frightening her with a boy she doesn't even know.'

After Blanche had gone I looked across. Curtains open, but no swan on her window sill. Then I knew something was up.

She only opened her door a crack. 'Oh, Birdie,' she said, 'I thought you'd never get here,' and then she started. I've never seen Clarice cry before. All the troubles she's had and she's always been so cheerful.

As soon as I got inside I could smell the paint. And see it. Great peach footprints all over her hall mat and across her living room.

I said, 'I came as soon as I couldn't see your swan. I thought your helper hadn't turned up.'

'No,' she said, 'she's been. But they broke the swan. Knocked it over and broke its neck. And wait till you see what they've done to my bedroom.' It looked like a troupe of monkeys had been in there with paint brushes. Peach emulsion everywhere. Over the wallpaper, except they'd missed patches, and where there was anything in the way, like her little dressing-table mirror, they'd just painted round it, and over the woodwork, all in dribbles and runs. It was on the floor, on the bed, on the curtains and the glass.

I said, 'I thought you were going to tell that teacher you weren't interested?'

She said, 'I was, Birdie, but he didn't come back. They just turned up with the paint. Three girls. Great big girls. And I hadn't seen a shade card or anything.'

I said, 'Didn't you tell them to go away?'

'Well,' she said, 'I did try. But they said it was all arranged, and they'd get in trouble if they didn't do it for their Community Awareness. And they were such big girls, Birdie.'

Of course Clarice is shrinking. I made her some

tea and had a go at the carpet with a damp cloth, but it was slow work.

She said, 'They were only here till twelve. They didn't wipe down or anything. Just straight in with the paint, and I don't even like the colour. It's a horrible colour. And then at twelve they said they were going for chips, and they never came back. I've had to put their brushes and everything in my bathroom because I didn't know what else to do with them.'

I said, 'What was that teacher's name?' She thought it might have been Swallow, but she couldn't be sure. Didn't matter. Clark'd know who he was. She did look beaten. I told her Wilf'd be more than happy to come and put things right. Hang a bit of wallpaper and clean things up. Wilf loves a project.

'No,' she said, 'I don't want any more bother. I'll live with it. If you could just help me get rid of the paint pots, and rub the worst of it off the carpets.'

'Birdie,' she said, when I was leaving, 'I've been thinking, perhaps I will get the phone put in. I've got a bit in the savings bank, for my funeral, but I'm getting that I don't really care. Would four thousand two hundred pounds be enough? As long as I wasn't talking on it for hours?'

'Spend it, you noggin,' I said. 'Look after yourself. Just imagine, get your phone connected up, on your bedside table, any colour you like, then any problems you can ring me or Blanche or anybody. No more signalling with swans.'

She said, 'Is your funeral paid for?'

Not likely. I've told Wilf he can roll me up in a bin liner and use me as a Gro-bag. I asked her if she wanted me to try and get her another swan, but she said she'd never really liked it. She said she wouldn't mind a candelabra, if ever I saw one on my travels. A gold-coloured one, with red candles. There's more to Clarice than meets the eye. I can see it'll be like that Ivana Trump's place over there once she starts spending. That helper'll come in one morning to peel her a grape, and there'll be Clarice, draped on a bedspread made from three kinds of fur.

Jimmy didn't turn up. Didn't bother me. I would have done my roots anyway.

I asked Clark if there was a teacher at Aldersbrook called Sparrow or Starling or Spoonbill, or something like, but the only She could think of was Miss Slaughter, who took them for computers. I said, 'What are you doing for this Community Awareness week, then?' He said they were painting a mural on the side of the leisure centre. People running and jumping and chucking balls, and Welcome written all over it. In Gujarati, and everything under the sun bar English, if I know anything about it. When I asked down the health centre for a pamphlet for Clarice about having someone come round to do your feet, they gave me one for people from Vietnam. I got all the way up to Cherry Tree before I realized. This is why we're in the mess we're in. Paring corns for the whole wide world.

He said, 'And I've got to write about somebody I

know who's done something interesting. Do you know anybody?'

I said, 'What kind of interesting?'

'Been on telly,' he said, 'or shipwrecked or anything.'

I said, 'How about Wilf? You know, my friend who brings me all those veggies.'

He said, 'Yeah, all right. What's he done?'

I said, 'He was in the D-Day landings, is what he's done. Went ashore at Arromanches, and then he was in Germany and Holland getting shot to pieces. He'd have been in Burma as well if they hadn't dropped the big bomb. Or what about Clarice? That you took the ham for yesterday? She got the Royal Red Cross, and you didn't get that for knitting socks. We were all in the war, you know. We've all got tales to tell. Even Olive.'

He said, 'Which war was that? I've seen about Desert Storm. We won.'

That's about the size of it. We're just ancient history now. All those lads, not much older than Clark, that never came back. Blue Catlin copped it at Anzio. He was a good-looker. Lovely big shoulders on him. And the Brocks boys. One lost at Tobruk, another one went down with the *Newfoundland*, and the only one that came home was a bag of bones by the time the Japs had finished with him.

Then he said, 'There's Mr Swift. He begins with S. Why do you want to know?'

I didn't let on. I didn't want it all over the play-ground that some old lizard was on the warpath. But I did mention it to Olive when I saw her.

'You be careful, Birdie,' she said. 'Get those big girls in trouble and your life won't be worth living.' I did think I might get Wilf to go with me, for a bit of moral support, but there was no sign of him. Probably down the allotments. You can never find a man when you need one.

I thought the thing to do was get down there just before they finish for dinner, before the stampede, and then wait for him. The woman in the office said if I didn't have an appointment she couldn't guarantee he'd see me. She said if I wanted to risk it I could sit and wait. Sitting on her fat backside, shuffling papers and talking to me through the glass. I said, 'Is that bullet-proof?' Pretended she hadn't heard me.

Then a young man came along and smiled at me. He asked me if I was being helped, and when I asked him if he could get this Mr Swift bing-bonged, he said what he'd do was, as soon as the bell went for break, he'd catch him in the staff room and ask him to pop along. The paper-shuffler didn't like that.

'Oh, headmaster,' she said, 'I already explained to the lady about making an appointment.'

When that bell went, nothing happened. For about ten seconds nothing happened, and then this shaking started, a rumbling and then a thundering. It was like somebody had opened the pens down the livestock market. Great herds of them, all black and white, with their shirts hanging out and rings through their noses, swinging their bags arid kicking each other in the privates and shouting and hollering. The thing that amazed me was how many of them were in there. The number of them I'd seen ducking and diving round the Fruit Bowl, writing on walls and up to no good, I should have thought the classrooms would be empty.

So then it all went quiet and Mrs Wobble Bottom behind the glass put her coat on and gave me a look. I'd be sitting there yet if I hadn't stopped a little sprat coming out of the girls' toilets and asked her where the staff room was.

I don't know if you're supposed to knock. It's a long time since I was at school. I gave the door a tap and nobody came, so in I went, and I couldn't see a hand in front of my face for the smoke. A woman said, 'I'm afraid you can't come in here.'

I said, 'I don't want to, not without a respirator. Is there a man in here beginning with S?'

I'd forgotten his name again. I can remember things from 1932. The principal tributaries of the Yorkshire Ouse are the Swale, the Ure, the Nidd, the Wharf, the Ayr, the Calder and the Don. She was an old besom that took us for geography. 'Only imbeciles lean their handwriting backwards,' she used to say, and then, Whack! that ruler'd come down across your knuckles. Joy and peace to you too, Miss Bates. These days, if you're left-handed you can get special scissors and everything.

I said, 'I've been waiting half an hour to see the man who's been sending kids out, painting people's houses.' So then she went and found him for me. Tubby little type, very heavy on his feet.

He said, 'Community Awareness Week's finished. You'll have to wait till next year.'

I said, 'What do you think you're at? Sending a bunch of comedians into an old lady's flat, wreaking havoc.'

'Now hang on,' he said.

I said, 'No. I'll hang on in a minute, when I've finished telling you the trouble you've caused.' They were all listening then, sitting there in the smog with their sandwich boxes. So I told him about poor Clarice, with paint all over her carpet and her swan broken. I said, 'And she didn't even want her flat painted. She liked it how it was.'

He said, 'Well, she must have agreed to it, otherwise I wouldn't have sent them. We can only do a certain number, you know? We can't get round to everybody.'

I said, 'Well, I'm glad to hear it. But that doesn't help Clarice. She's got peach paint everywhere, bar the bits of wall they couldn't reach, and her nerves are shot to pieces. She was shaking when I went over there, trembling all over. She's frightened those girls might come back.'

'No,' he said, 'you've got it all wrong. As I recall, she was a very nervy old lady anyway. Didn't seem to understand we were doing her a favour. Free decorating. Maybe I should have explained it a bit more, but I only have so much time. People like you coming in complaining makes me wonder why we even bother. But you can tell her there won't be anybody coming back. Awareness Week's finished.'

I said, 'When does Cleaning Up An Old Lady's Carpet Week start?'

He said, 'I must say you're making a lot of fuss about this. It's only emulsion. It'll come off with a damp cloth. They're only kids, you know? You can't expect a professional job from kids. And free as well.'

I said, 'I shall be writing to the papers about this.' I shan't, though. What's the point? They never get their facts straight, and Clarice wouldn't want her name in the paper, not even if they spelled it wrong.

HELPING HANDS

Pensioners and other disadvantaged groups on the Fruit Bowl and Clover Farm estates have been benefiting from a Community Awareness Week organised by Aldersbrook Comprehensive.

Says head of Pastoral Studies, Colin Swift, 'Pupils have been out gardening and decorating for those worse off than themselves. Research shows that this kind of project really raises awareness and helps the youngsters to see senior citizens as real people.'

Other activites have been mural-painting, childminding, and creating a web site with interesting stories about local people.

Madonna Givens, 13, said, 'We did some weeding and helped at a play-group. I think it's a good thing for old people to get visited, otherwise they won't know what's going on in the world.'

'We have had excellent feedback,' says Mr Switt.

'I think the kids would have been
happy to carry on, but we've got the
National Curriculum to think about.'

I saw that Jen on my way back from Aldersbrook. Overtook her, as a matter of fact. She walks so slow it's a wonder she stays upright. It's a wonder the force of gravity doesn't get her. Just been to her circle dancing group, she told me. She said, 'You should come along some time. It's very gentle. We did a lovely one today from Bulgaria.'

I said, 'I'm looking for a place I can get a nice quickstep.'

'Oh,' she says, 'aren't you a marvel. I hope I'm half as good as you when I'm your age.' She won't be. Carrying too much blubber. She'll be long gone. I told her I used to be out dancing five nights a week. Leytonstone Regal, Barking Astoria, Ilford Palais.

'Marvellous,' she said. That woman smiles too much. She said they'd been doing something from Ghana as well, getting in touch with the earth. I've seen some of them going into the leisure centre, wafting along in those long skirts Mrs Kumar sells down the market. Not a brassiere between them, and they never shave their legs. It's funny. You get to about fifty and the hair on your legs just gives up growing. You don't have to bother shaving any more, even if you're wearing pop socks. Course, you start needing a good pair of tweezers – for your chin.

I said, 'Are the men any good?'

'Oh,' she said, 'we don't allow men.' So now I know she's crackers.

The lifts were working – glory be and alleluia – but I had to get out at level five because I couldn't stand the smell. I rapped on Olive's door as I was passing, to see if she'd heard any more about winning that car.

'You've had a man round looking for you,' she said. Everybody knows your business in the Fruit Bowl.

I said, 'Did he have a dog?'

'No,' she said. 'He'd got one of those mobile phones.'

No news on the car, but she's gone in for another contest to win a Gameboy. She thinks it'd help her Brian pass the hours.

I told her about Clarice's carpet and the teacher and everything. 'Waste of time,' she said. 'I don't know why you bothered. Nobody cares when you're old. Anyway, Clarice ought to be in a home. We all should. Somewhere with handrails on the bath. Then they could do something with these flats.' Dynamite them. And bags I push the plunger.

Olive thinks we should all clear out and let the homeless move in. She thinks we've had our time, but I'm still having mine.

I'd been in ten minutes. Just had my Milky Way and a Guinness and there was somebody at my door. Great big black boy with a hairstyle. I've seen him around.

He said, 'Afternoon, lady. You bin gettin' trouble, is it, from next door?' Snake Eye hadn't been back since the night I fetched the police out, and Dawn's no trouble. As long as she's got her temazepam I don't hear a peep out of her.

He said he was from the council, but he never was. Nice silky windcheater, £100 plimsolls. He gave me a card, A1 Neighbourhood Security, but nothing with a photo on, like they're supposed to have from the housing department or gas or anything like that. Then he said he was sub-contracted by the council, and if I had any bother to phone that number. Said the idea was to save us calling the law every time there was a bit of bother along the landings.

'Nice lady like you,' he said, 'don't want no trouble, know what I mean? Don't want to be wasting police time, is it?'

Leaning on my doorpost like that, sucking his teeth. I wished Wilf'd come along with a bit of beetroot or something. They always change their tune if they think there's a man about. It wasn't even a proper card. The name wasn't even on straight.

I said, 'Is this coming out of my council tax?' It could have been. They're always dreaming up enterprise schemes, trying to get some of these wasters out of bed in the morning. I sent an idea in once, about giving them a wake-up call with a hosepipe of cold water, and they wrote back and said my suggestion had been duly noted.

He never answered me about the council tax. Just stood there, trying to see into my flat. I hadn't hardly seen a black man till 1944, then me and Pearl went to the Rainbow Corner one night. I danced with a boy from Oklahoma, 'where the wind comes sweepin' down the plain', and Pearl ended up with a medical orderly from Baltimore, black as your hat and perfect teeth. She said he was exactly the same as a white man, but I don't know how far she checked. She copped it not long after that, from a buzz bomb.

He said, 'I could check you security, lady. Get one of my men, fix up you locks and stuff.' Dwayne. That's his name. Lives in Almond Blossom, with zinc sheeting nailed across his windows.

I said, 'I've got locks.' I've got a little table I put

across the front door at night, as well, leg them over if they try breaking in, and a bag of pepper and a little alarm thing Olive got out of a catalogue – makes enough noise to waken the dead if you put a battery in it.

'Any bother,' he said, 'we be here in five minutes, two minutes. Be safe, lady.'

He was just going when Jimmy turned up with the dog. She was leaping up at that Dwayne like he was a long-lost friend, trying to lick his face.

'Call it off,' he shouts. 'Call it off. I got dog allergy.' Ask me, it was his fancy jacket he was worried about.

Jimmy said, 'Put your curlers in. I'm taking you out tonight.'

Wait long enough your luck has to change. Not that I wear curlers. Heated rollers, I've got, and mousse, and when all else fails a nice little champagne-blond wig from Selfridge's sale, but not in the summer. I don't know what it's made of, but half an hour under it and you could run a turbine off the steam. Tights. That was my only problem. I don't bother with them except for funerals. So I sent him down to Kareem's Kabin while me and Vanessa shared a Double Decker, and he was gone that long I nearly called out the Mounties. Navy, he came back with, navy thirty denier. That's what happens when you send a man shopping.

I said, 'Are we going up West?'

He said he wanted it to be a surprise, but how are you supposed to know what to wear? Especially if it's dancing. If we were going to be sitting in the pictures I could wear those black courts that cripple me. But if we were going dancing I'd definitely need my old faithfuls, with the leather snipped a little bit to ease my bunions. I don't like surprises.

I said, 'What about your dog?'

'Ah,' he said, 'I was wondering. She's as good as gold. You wouldn't know you'd got her.'

Of course the council don't allow pets. Only budgies and goldfish. There's a few of them round here got those dogs that have to have their head kept in a basket. Ugly-looking animals that have your hand off if you make a sudden move, so they must be breaking the rules. And there's three-legged mongrels hoppity skipping everywhere – all had arguments with cars – but nobody knows who any of them belong to. And then there was a story once that someone in Cherry Tree had got an alligator; just a little baby thing, but then it got bigger and turned nasty, so they flushed it down the lav. I don't know if it was true, but for a long time after, Clarice wouldn't have the lid left up on her toilet, and Olive still won't. She thinks it might come swimming up into Apple Bough and take a chunk out of her.

Jimmy said he'd got a bit of business to attend to, back in Brighton. He said it'd be easier to leave her with me than take her with him.

I said, 'I bet she'd love a run on the beach. I know I would.' It wasn't that I didn't want to have her.

He said he'd look upon it as a very great favour and it'd only be for a day or two. A week at most. 'Anyway,' he said, 'then Frank'll be back from Malta.'

I said, 'I thought he was in Tenerife?'

'Same thing,' he said. 'And she's not a dog that's been mollycoddled. Boiled tripe and a bit of straw bedding in an outhouse, that's all she's used to.'

So I said she could stay, but no more than two nights and I wasn't boiling tripe for anybody. Then I made him take her out for a run round the block. Give me five minutes to do something with my

Creme-Puff. And just as he was going, Wilf turned up with a few tomatoes.

He said, 'They'll need ripening on your window sill, but they should be all right. I didn't know you'd got visitors.' He was eyeing Jimmy and Jimmy was eyeing him.

Jimmy said, 'Real tomatoes? Blimey, Birdie, when you were married to me, if it didn't come in a tin you didn't want to know.'

There was no need for Wilf to look at me that way. He knew I'd had husbands.

We got Vanessa settled all right. Daft name for a dog. And for an animal that's always slept in out-houses she soon got the hang of my settee.

He said he wanted it to be a surprise, but when we got to Stratford and he had me running to catch the 158, I smelled a rat. 'Go on,' he said, 'wave your arm. They'll wait for a woman. Tell them I'm disabled.' It was a young girl driving; three earrings all in one ear. I wouldn't have minded a job like that myself, but when the boys came home after the end of the war we had to stand aside. When there's a war on they're happy for you to do anything. Afterwards they want you to learn shorthand and typing.

She said, 'You needn't have run. I'm just going on my break.'

So there we sat for twenty minutes, with the windows too smeared to see out, and Jimmy ferreting around for his angina tablets. I said, 'So we're not going dancing?'

He said, 'With my heart?'

I said, 'What then? The pictures?' I wouldn't have minded seeing that *Jurassic Park*, but nobody else wanted to. Wilf says he can't sit all that time. He gets bored and his leg twitches if he doesn't keep on the move. And Blanche and Olive like videos. Put them in a little machine and then watch them on Blanche's telly. They reckon it's safer than walking home from the Warner in the dark – but you can go in the daytime. They have matinées, and Clark told me they have food and popcorn and all sorts. He said there's even a special holder in the arm of your seat, in case you have a drink. And if you fetch a video you've still got to walk home. The pond life you see in that shop, they could follow you and grab your purse. They'd have the skin off your back, some of them, if it'd buy them a few pills.

Three or four times a week we used to go to the pictures. Specially if it was Robert Mitchum. I loved the way he lit a cigarette.

I said, 'Are we going to Walthamstow?' I knew we were. I said, 'You could have told me. Surprises. I wouldn't have sent you out buying tights and coming back with the wrong colour if I'd known we were only going to the dogs.'

'Now you've spoilt it,' he said. 'But we'll have to go. I've paid for the tickets.' I thought, I wouldn't have bothered with scent if I'd known I was going to be standing in the Popular at Stow, squashed in with some of those armpits. But blow me down if he didn't wheel me into the Paddock Grill.

I said, 'Have you seen these prices?'

'You have whatever you want,' he said. 'My treat. Have a T-bone. Have a prawn cocktail.' Of course I never was a big eater. I said, 'Have you come into money?'

He said, 'I do all right. Do a few little jobs, cash in hand. Got a nice little flat, all paid off. You could come down and see it some time. Stop for a bit. We rubbed along all right before.'

We didn't. It was dogs, dogs, everlasting dogs. You could never go dancing because they were always working nights. Even in the blackout. They used to race them in the afternoon then, but dog people have always got a hundred things to do down at the kennels. They're never finished for the day. That's why I started going on my own. And that's how I came to meet Number Two. It was Hitler's doing that I met Jimmy, and Jimmy's doing that I met Berto, and way leads on to way. It did make me think, though, about going down there. Fresh air, no more broken lifts, split the telly licence fifty-fifty.

Jimmy said he'd got the name of a sure thing in the second race, but there's no such animal.

I took a flyer on the Larry Herbert Memorial Puppy Stakes. Lady-Be-Good. Jimmy shook his head when he saw what I'd picked, but she came home at 12/1 and his was left for dead. After that it was just money thrown away. I couldn't find myself a winner, didn't matter what system I tried. And he kept disappearing. Said it was bladder trouble, but I spotted him a couple of times, ducking and diving around by the bookies. Then, last race but one, I did a reverse forecast on Choccy-Woccy and Starburst. £54. Thank you and good night.

I said, 'I'm not running for any more buses. I'm spending some of this on a mini-cab.'

I had a bit of trouble with wandering hands in the back of the car, but I soon put a stop to that. The Paddock Grill's very nice, but it's not that nice. Scampi in a basket and men think you're anybody's.

I said, 'Where do you want dropping?'

'Oh,' he said, 'I thought perhaps?'

But my settee was already spoken for.

'First date, Jimmy,' I said. 'What kind of a girl do you take me for?'

He said, 'You're a hard woman, Bird.'

He got out in Stratford Broadway, so I never did see where he was staying. He promised he'd be back for Vanessa, Saturday at the latest. He promised faithfully.

There's three different types of hooligans on the Fruit Bowl. The Bloods are the boys, and the Grievers are some other boys that come over from the Clover Farm Estate. Then there are the Billies; they're the girls. The boys aren't too much trouble to somebody like me, because apart from spraying paint on walls and playing big loud wirelesses they mainly just fight each other and thieve cars. Then they crash them because they don't know how to drive, and there's been one or two of them wiped out that way – only fourteen or fifteen years old. At least they haven't had time to breed. Wilf says they could all do with two years' National Service, get them out of those baggy trousers and learning to stand up straight, but Blanche says there's more to it than that. She says they run errands for people who're real trouble. She means people like Dwayne, and somebody in Orange Grove that sells the wacky baccy. That's why she makes Clark go to Sunday school, to try and keep him on the straight and narrow.

Almond Blossom is the worst, no doubt about it. There's comings and goings over there all night long, and it isn't just tarts. There is two of them at that old business over there, and I know that for certain. But there's other carryings-on as well. Stuff going in, stuff coming out. Hot property. And little packages. And the arguments. Neighbours, domestics. There was a woman over there, up on the top floor, had a row with her boyfriend and cut his ear off. Chucked it over her walkway. They had police down there searching with flashlights, one of those deep-freeze bags at the ready, but they never did find it. Dogs had it, probably.

That's what it's like over there, till three and four in the morning. Then it goes quiet. Safest time to be out round here is early in the morning. You can meet some nasty individuals along these landings, but at least they don't get up before twelve.

But it's the Billies I don't like. There's a big crowd of them. Some of them are just hangers-on, young ones, just learning all their tricks, but there's about ten of the main morons, and they're bigger than any of the lads, and harder. Tamsin's the big cheese. I remember her when she was seven. Pushed a breeze-block off Orange Grove onto a police car and missed a WPC by inches. Nothing ever came of it. They said she was too young. They said they didn't have a proper case against her. And now she's got a whole crowd of no-necks following her about, think she's the queen bee.

So I'd just taken Vanessa for a breath of air, only down to the health centre to fetch Clarice's prescription, then back along Blackberry Hedge. Now there's a road that's hit the skids. Years back, when Wilf Orme first asked me to get wed, I did think about it because we'd have qualified for a little maisonette along there, only two storeys high and your own patch of garden, but it's all rusty old bangers now and half of it's boarded up. One of them's a squat advice centre. I sometimes wonder why I bother paying rent.

There were some Billies hanging about outside Apple Bough, standing right in my way when I tried to get in the lift. One of them said, 'That's a greyhound. They're dead fast.' I held on tight to her lead.

She said, 'Does she bite?'

I said, 'Oh yes.' But of course milady was nuzzling up to her, looking for sweets. Looking to get her ears scratched.

She said, 'Where do you live?' I wasn't telling her where I lived. So then she shouted up to one of the landings. I should have known there'd be more of them about somewhere. They go everywhere mob-handed.

It turned out a good thing the lift was jammed, because if I hadn't been dithering around, worrying about that big Tamsin with the scar down her face, I'd never have let go of Vanessa. She shot up the stairs, and when I got halfway up after her I had to stop and catch my breath. That was when I heard him crying. I looked up and there he was, hanging head down over the stairwell.

I couldn't think straight for a minute. I was worried they'd drop him, even if they didn't mean to. They're stupid enough. And there was no point knocking on anybody's door and asking them to give me a hand because I don't know anybody on level two, apart from Jinks, and he moves too slow for the human eye. I shouted, 'Hold on, Clark.' I don't know why. There wasn't anything for him to hold on to.

He didn't hear me anyway. He just kept crying, 'Don't drop me. Please don't.' Then I heard one of the Billies start screeching, 'Get it off me. Get it off.'

How I got up those stairs I shall never know. My running days are long gone. There were three of them, holding him by his feet, and Vanessa was jumping up at them. I suppose she thought it was a game.

I shouted, 'Pull him up. Get him up over that railing before she rips you to shreds.' She wouldn't know how to start. Anything bigger than Harold Hare is just a playmate to her, but it did the trick. They hauled him back, dropped him on the floor and legged it. I watched them from the edge of the walkway, the whole bunch of them heading across to the precinct in their big black anoraks, taking their time, laughing and joking. The one with the scar down her face turned round and saw me, and she pointed at me, like one of those cricket referees, as if to say, 'You've had it.' That's what they all say.

He was sobbing. He couldn't get his breath. 'My nan'll kill me,' he kept saying. I had to push him to get him moving. Banging on Blanche's door, I was, but of course she wasn't at home.

Olive heard me though, so out she came, too late for the action as usual. I told her what had happened.

'Oh, Clark,' she started. 'Your nan'll kill you.' I tried to give her the eye, stop her going on and upsetting him any more, but once Olive's up and running it's like trying to stop the Niagara Falls. Of course he'd gone in his trousers. Must have been the fear. But he was more bothered about the money than anything. A £10 note. He was supposed to fetch himself a pizza and get change for the electric meter.

I said, 'Is this another day off school?' He said he'd had a stomach ache, so his nan had kept him at home.

He said she'd had to go out, and he'd promised her he'd be all right.

We took him into Olive's and gave him a glass of orange. Then she rinsed his things through, and I took his key and fetched him a clean pair of trackies.

Vanessa wouldn't leave his side, but he was starting to perk up.

He said, 'She looks worried about me, Mrs Gibbs.'

Greyhounds always look worried. They've got their reasons.

Olive kept saying, 'Why ever did you tell them you had money, Clark? Now they'll be watching for you every time you go out.'

You don't need to tell the Billies you've got money. They just go through your pockets till they find it.

I said, 'Could happen to anybody, Olive. It's not Clark's fault. It could happen to you, how slow you walk.'

That shut her up. Sometimes she doesn't even remember to close her handbag. Waddling out of that post office with her purse just sitting there, might as well have a big sign round her neck says 'Mug Me'.

I said, 'What happened about that composition you've got to write for school. About somebody who's done something interesting?'

'Done it,' he said. 'I've done it about Mr Orme. He told me all about D-Day. I'll probably get a merit mark for it. He came to our flat for a cup of thundering char, That's what they call it in the Army. And he brought my nan a box of Milk Tray.'

Did he indeed.

Olive said, 'You could have asked me. I had a war too, you know?'

She did. She was a spark-plug tester first, then a riveter, and then she ended up in the ATS. She was a tracker on the searchlight crews. You wouldn't think it to look at her now – bad legs, bad eyes. She fetched some photos out to show Clark: a big crowd of them that worked on the Lancasters, and one of her with her first husband, her in her khaki stockings, him with a big smile.

She said, 'We'd only been married five months when I got the telegram, and they stopped me eleven shillings out of his money for the blanket they buried him in.'

Clark said, 'I know about shillings. That's fifty-five pee in real money. What's my nan going to say about the electric meter?'

Olive said she'd keep him till Blanche got back. He was happy going through her old photos.

I said, 'They're getting worse, those Billies. One slip and he'd have gone head first. I've got a good, mind to report it.'

'You don't want to do that,' she said. 'It'll only bring more trouble.'

She's right, of course.

She said, 'I hear your other half turned up.'

I couldn't think what she meant for a minute.

'You needn't act dumb with me,' she said. 'Everybody knows.'

Me and Vanessa went home and we had two Mars bars, cut up into slices. I've never been anybody's other half. And Clark could have written about me.

They think it was all blowing up bridges and shooting and wriggling along the ground with half a tree stuck to your helmet, but there was a lot more to the war effort than that. Min Talbot's sister worked in the munitions. Got three fingers blown off and her face turned yellow. And Rene's sister was in the WAAF. She was the girl that made the thing that drills the hole that holds the spring. We all were.

That Jen came visiting. She said, 'I've brought you some mint tea bags, because if you're anything like me you've got too much yang this time of year.'

There's always something with her. She's getting to be such a size, and I can't understand why. Grapefruit; that's all I ever see in her shopping bag. Grapefruit and crispbreads. And still she gets bigger, so maybe it is this yang she's filling up with. I've no experience of it, myself. I'm the same round my waist as when I was seventeen, and I've never had minty tea in my life.

She said, 'I'm in a mess, Birdie. I've got to get back in touch with myself.' She'd got a ten-point plan.

I said, 'I'll tell you what I'd do. I'd have a one-point plan, and that'd be, get as far away from this place as I could go. Young woman like you. Why don't you pack your bags? Get yourself a nice little job somewhere and start over?'

'No,' she said. 'When I got together with Flick, we were agreed. We wanted to get away from smug suburban values. We want to live among *real* people.'

I said, 'Well you've definitely done that. We've got real thieves here, real vandals. If it's scum of the earth you're after, we've got the genuine article here. There was even a real eviction over there yesterday, I hear.'

The bailiff's men had come to get the Warriners out – never paid their rent in years, and according to what I heard there was doggy business everywhere. Wall to wall. Olive had a grandstand view, and she said the council men had masks over their noses when they went in afterwards, and overalls and rubber gloves.

She said, 'The main thing is, you've got to really focus on the things that used to make you happy.'

Like men raising their hat to you in the street. I miss that. She said she'd bought herself some wax crayons, and she was thinking of getting herself a kite. Definitely a screw or two loose there.

'And don't tell anybody,' she said, 'but I've been howling as well, in our kitchen. It helps unblock you. Howling and stamping.'

Her secret's safe with me.

Snake Eye's back. I heard Dawn shouting the odds, and there's only one reason she ever does that. They say if you have kids you stand by them whatever they do. I'm glad I never had to put that to the test. They say kids are a comfort to you when you get old, but I can't see it. Olive's Brian's only two miles down the road and months go by without him visiting. He says he can't manage the stairs, but that needn't stop him having her over for her Sunday dinner. She'd love that. Making a crumble to take with her, and helping with the washing up. That'd be right up Olive's alley.

Wilf's got a daughter, married and everything, and she does phone him, but they're up in Bootle and I don't ever remember them visiting. He sends them a gift voucher at Christmas, and they send him one back.

Clarice phoned. She wanted a bottle of sherry as well as her usual stuff. Spend, spend, spend. There's no stopping her since she had that telephone put in. She said to me, 'What's a fax, Birdie?' It was something she'd seen in a brochure. She said, 'Do you think I should get one?'

I thought I'd take Vanessa with me, give her a run down to the allotments and see what was bugging Wilf. I hadn't seen hide nor hair of him since the day he bumped into Jimmy. And talking of disappearing acts, Jimmy hadn't showed his face again either. Left me holding the baby, and it's thirty-two pence a tin for Scoundrel. Not that I mind having her. She's no trouble, and she did save Clark's life, more or less, which is what we're all agreed we should tell the council if they start giving me bell, book and candle about keeping pets. But she's making herself at home here, and sooner or later she's got to go back to sleeping in an outhouse somewhere. And another thing about it is, if I was to keep her, say Dwyer never comes back, I definitely think I'd change her name. I definitely think I'd call her Flake, because those are her favourites. Not that I am going to keep her. I'm too old to start a family.

Wilf wasn't out hoeing or raking or whatever it is he does down there, but I could see his shed door was open. Course, everybody stopped what they were doing to give me the once over. Never a smile or a hello. Probably thought I was going to vandalize somebody's sprouts, jump on somebody's radishes, do the whole world a favour. It could have been my leopard-skin leggings, though. They're only made from Lycra, but anything that looks like it came off an animal people give you the evil eye these days.

So there they were, inside his shed, with a Thermos of tea and two little folding chairs. I said, 'What's this, the Ritz?'

'Birdie,' she said, 'you gave me a fright. I've just been helping Wilf with a bit of weeding.'

He said, 'Like a few beans, Birdie? Or a lettuce?'

I said, 'I never took you for a gardener, Blanche.'

'Oh yes,' she said, 'I love it. You come down here and you feel like you're a million miles away from those flats. Peace and quiet.'

'Fresh air,' he said.

'Fresh veggies,' she said.

They sounded like Bill and Ben the Flower Pot Men. They sounded like Dr Carrot and Potato Pete. 'Eat carrots,' they used to say to us, 'and see in the dark like Cat's-Eyes Cunningham.' He was a pilot on the night raids; second to none. Ask me, though, he got more help from the radar than he did from eating any carrots.

I said, 'Clark all right? No more trouble from those Billies?'

'No,' she said, 'but he's still off school with his stomach. I think it could be his nerves.'

I think it could be all those greens he's not used to.

I said, 'I'll maybe see you later, Wilf? Help you clear up a bit round by the bins?'

'No thank you,' he said. 'Me and Blanche did it this morning.'

Doesn't bother me. I've got plenty to do without playing Boy Scouts with Wilf Orme. And if he's got the hump because of Jimmy Dwyer, that's his lookout. If he wants to make a fool of himself with a younger woman, let him. He won't go out anywhere, sitting in, reading his gardening books. She'll find out. It'll be a five-minute wonder. Then she'll be back at her bingo and Clark's guts'll stop troubling him.

Clarice said, 'Who's upset you?'

Just because I didn't want a sherry didn't mean I was upset.

She said, 'A man came to see me this morning. Brought me something. I'll think what it was in a minute.'

That's how she's getting these days, since she got the extra telly channels. She sits and watches anything. Aerobics. Fishing. Shopping At Night.

I said, 'Was it that reverend?' I could see the magazine he brings her lying there on the side.

'I don't think so,' she said. 'He was as black as your hat.'

I said, 'Don't you wish you could get away from here? Live somewhere nice, like normal people?'

It doesn't get her down like it does me. It's a rare thing to find Clarice not smiling, sitting there with her blanket round her knees. She's got a very contented nature. And she's in her own little world inside that flat, looking at her big calendar with pictures of Switzerland. She's got a little table she can swivel round in front of her. Prayer book, remote for the telly and a special box for all her tablets. I'm the one has to go pushing and shoving round the Wavy Line. I suppose the thing is, Clarice never did get out much, even when she could.

She said, 'You're not going to leave, are you?'

I said, 'If the right chance came along I'd be off.'

'Oh no, Birdie,' she said. 'Don't say so. Whatever would I do if you left?'

I think Blanche'd do her shopping for her, if it came to it, which it won't, because I wouldn't live with Jimmy Dwyer again, not if you paid me in big gold bars.

I said, 'I'm not going anywhere.'

'Locks,' she said. 'That's what the black man came about. He can put locks on your windows for a good price, and there's a number you can phone too, if you get any trouble. He said they could be here faster than a police car.'

I spotted his card on the side when I put her sherry away. A1 Security.

I said, 'I thought we agreed you wouldn't let people in?'

She said, 'He was in and out in no time. And very polite. I did talk to him with my chain still across when he first knocked, but he couldn't check my windows like that, could he? Not if I didn't let him in.'

She'll end up a statistic, that woman.

Wilf was out at the side of Orange Grove, trying to scrub off some new writing. We haven't talked much lately. 'Look at this,' he said. 'Flaming eyesore. And it doesn't even say anything.'

It's true. There's things sprayed all over the estate, and you can't read any of it. Blanche says it's graffiti, but it just looks like squiggle, squiggle, squiggle to me.

He said, 'I might go down the council depot. See if I can get some steel wool. Are you coming with me?' So then I knew we were still friends. But I'd got errands to run: Clarice's shopping, Olive's prescription and twenty ciggies for Patti along the landing, because she'd got to wait in for her social worker.

'I don't know, Birdie,' he said, 'we're supposed to be retired, you and me, and yet sometimes I think we're the only ones still working.' I told him I'd see him later, give him a hand.

'You're a star,' he said. 'I think I'll take a little jam jar as well, see if they've got any paint stripper.'

I knew that'd be a wasted journey. All they've got down that depot is a bunch of time-servers and a lot of cream paint. You can have any colour scheme, as long as it's cream gloss. I came back about eleven, and there he was, scraping away in his washing-up gloves. He'd forked out his own money.

'Something wrong here, Wilf,' I said. 'They buy these paint cans with money they haven't earned, spray it all over, as if this place isn't ugly enough already, and then you spend your pension money putting things back to rights.'

'I know,' he said. 'But I can't walk past this every day, as if it doesn't matter. Start thinking like that and we might as well all move into a piggery and be done with it.'

I took over for a bit to give his arm a rest, and that Jen went past. Never offered to help. 'You two are marvellous for your age,' she said. They like it if you're marvellous for your age. If you can't be that they want you down Plaistow Crematorium, not hanging about here, taking up bus seats.

Wilf said, 'What this place needs is trees.' He's only

been on the Fruit Bowl six years. He didn't see it how it used to be.

I said, 'We had trees, and there's no prizes for guessing what happened to them.'

He said, 'Doesn't mean they couldn't try again. People might appreciate them more this time. I'm writing to the council. I've had this idea. They could turn that patch down between Almond Blossom and Apple Bough into a proper little garden. Maybe even get a couple of seats put in. A garden improves people.'

We scrubbed till twelve, and it was starting to look better. He said, 'Come down the Tuck-In. I reckon we deserve it.' Tuesdays, Wednesdays and Thursdays they do a pensioner special: soup, bread and a proper pudding for a pound. I'm not big on soup and Wilf's not big on puddings, so we make a good pair.

He said, 'It was like a mothers' meeting in that depot. Warm as toast, and men hanging around drinking tea, and this big surly type at the counter. He said nothing goes out of there without a pink docket. So I said I'd go up to Housing and get one. Then he said they didn't have any stripper anyway, nor steel wool. So what kind of a building stores is that? I don't think he knows what he has got. Pink dockets! I told him I was doing the council a favour, getting rid of vandalism. And he said it wasn't council policy. No money for it. Little Hitler.'

I was trying to remember that song. 'There was cheese, cheese, wafting on the breeze, in the stores . . .'

We had to stop while he thought. 'Can't rack my brain and walk at the same time,' he said. 'Not on an empty stomach.' Then he got it. 'There was ham, ham, mixed up with the jam, in the stores. There were flies, flies, feeding off the pies, and eggs, eggs, nearly growing legs, in the stores, in the stores . . .'

So we sang it all the way across to the Tuck-In, and I saw one of that Jen's droopy dancing friends heading towards us. I said, 'And we don't want you telling us we're marvellous.' That wiped the smile off her face.

Wilf had two oxtail soups, and I had two jam roll and custards, and he drew a plan on his serviette of how he pictured this little garden.

'Camellias,' he said. 'They'd do well. And a lilac and a witch hazel, and a few roses. Then we could have crocuses in the grass, so they just pop up. Autumn ones and spring ones, and snowdrops as well.'

I said, 'Who's going to pay for all this?'

He was quiet for a bit. He said, 'We'll try the council first. And if they say no, we'll go to the *Herald*. Get a campaign going.' I don't know who this *we* is he keeps talking about.

He went over to the allotments afterwards, to have a look at his compost heap, so I walked back on my own, past Orange Grove, to see how it was looking. Blow me down if they weren't back with their spray cans. Three of those boys that run around for Big Dwayne. I shouted at them but it didn't come out very loud. I was too stuffed with jam roll. They looked at me like I'd just landed from the moon.

I said, 'What do you think you're at? Mr Orme just cleaned that.'

They shuffled about a bit. One of them said, 'We just be chilling.'

I said, 'Looks to me like you're spraying.' They wear these daft red things round their heads, so everybody'll know which bunch of retards they belong to.

'It's we turf,' he said. They can't even talk. It's no wonder all they can spray is squiggle, squiggle, squiggle.

I said, 'Why have you all got hankies on your heads?'

'Ain't no hanky,' he said. 'It's we colours. So we get respeck from people.'

The Bloods, that's what they're called. That other lot, the Grievers, wear those American baseball hats, but with the peak round the side. Half-wits. Olive says they sniff ping-pong balls, and she could be right. There was one of them died last year – head in a carrier bag with a tin of lighter fuel. Nothing surprises me any more.

I said, 'Why do you want to go drawing on walls? Didn't your mum ever buy you colouring books?'

They laughed then. Thought I was some old waste of space no doubt.

'Naah,' he said. 'We just chilling.' They talk like that on these videos they watch. That's where they get it from. You can't say people don't learn anything from the telly.

He wouldn't tell me his name, but when I tried to get the can off him, he shouted, 'Bone,' to one of his mates and chucked it to him. They've all got names.

They started moving off, going somewhere else to spray, and the one called Bone was running backwards, shouting, 'Stay out of we business, lady. People don't stay out of we business, they get they windows busted in.'

We started clearing a patch for planting things. The council said there was no money available in the current spending round, but they'd consider the proposal again in the spring. But as Wilf said, we could all be dead and buried by the time they stir themselves. He said he'd pay for it himself. He said he'd talked to his Susan, because it'd have to come out of his savings and she might have expectations, but she'd told him to please himself with his money. Then a few of us chipped in, so there'd be enough for a seat as well – me, Blanche, Clarice, that Jen, Herbie and his wife, which was nice because she'll never get to sit on it, Nellie from the chemist's and the mad old Pole from Cherry Tree.

Herbie came down to give us a hand, lifting the turf and digging it over, and Wilf was back and forth from the allotment, fetching compost in his wheelbarrow.

The paper was meant to be sending somebody round at about eleven to take our photos and write up about it. Blanche had just brought us a Thermos down and we were taking a breather when who should come bowling round the corner but Jimmy Dwyer, searching for me, of course.

'Morning, girls,' he said. Wilf didn't even look at him.

Jimmy said, 'And how's my little sweetheart?'

I said, 'She's upstairs and she needs her nails clipping.'

Five weeks it had been.

I said, 'Your friend back yet from Majorca?'

'Yes,' he said, 'I've been meaning to come round, but you know how it is. Business. What's going on here, then?'

Wilf said, 'We're drilling for oil.'

Blanche said, 'You go, Birdie. Now you've got company, I'll stop and help Wilf.'

'Yes,' he said, 'you go. I've got Blanche and Herbie.'

Then they turned up from the *Herald*. One with his notepad and one with a big bag of cameras. Jimmy was in no hurry once he saw the cameras. He'd always loved having his picture taken. There were three Canadians we met down at Rottingdean during the war, and one of them took a picture of us – me, Pearl, and a girl from Croydon – and to this day I don't know how Dwyer got into that picture.

Of course Wilf did all the talking, trying to make sure they got their facts straight. If his mind hadn't been on that he'd never have let Jimmy be in the photo.

As soon as they'd finished Jimmy said, 'I could just borrow your key, save breaking up the party. I could just go up and get her.'

I gave him my spare key. Told him to leave it on the side on his way out, and take the tins and the doggy biscuits too.

He said, 'The thing is, we might be glad of you to have her again some time, know how I mean? So I could leave all that stuff.'

I said, 'Who's we?'

He said, 'Well, it's Frank really. He might be glad, you know, if he has to go away, and say I couldn't help out . . .'

Blanche kept saying, 'You go, Birdie. We can manage.' As if I was going to go running off upstairs with Jimmy Dwyer and leave her cosying up to Wilf and helping with the best bit: putting my magnolia in.

He said, 'I'll see you when you're not so busy. We could go up West. When's your best day?'

Hard to say really. Mondays it's the Savoy, Tuesdays it's the Café Royal. I said, 'Just don't come on a

Thursday. My feet never touch the ground.' I only go up to Stratford for a pensioner blow-dry and a mooch round the shops, but I still have Clarice to see to, and it'd be just my luck to miss a treat.

One thing about Jimmy, when he was in funds he was never shy about spending it on a girl. I saw him one time, after we split up. I was at Victoria station with a girl I worked with. We were on our way home and I ran smack into him. He was doing really well in those days. It was just after he'd won the Golden Collar at Catford, and he went across to the kiosk and bought me a big bar of Cadbury's. 'For old times' sake,' he said. He still had his teeth then. So did I, come to that.

He said, 'You feeling all right, Bird? I never thought I'd see you with a spade in your hand.' And then he went. The photographer was writing everybody's name down. He said, 'Who was the gent with the cigarette?'

Blanche said, 'A passing stranger.'

And Wilf said, 'Nobody. A delivery man. Can you rub him out?'

Of course they can. They can do anything with pictures – put flying saucers in, make you look like you're Slimmer of the Year, rewrite history. And if they can rub out one of those big Russians in a fur hat they wouldn't have any trouble getting rid of little Jimmy Dwyer.

Herbie said, 'I dare say you'll miss that dog now she's gone. We used to have a cocker spaniel years ago. Smashing company.'

I had got used to her. She liked to sit with me on the settee and share a Kit-Kat. And she loved a good tune. If I had the telly on she'd fall asleep, unless it was *Pet Rescue*, but the minute I put Woody Herman on, or the Squadronnaires, she'd be wide awake and listening.

Wilf said, 'Are we here to get these plants planted or is this Cruft's dog show?'

We'd got roses, Iceberg and Whisky Mac, as well as my tree still to put in.

He said, 'You do realize these don't grow very fast?' He'd only told me that every single day since I'd said I wanted a magnolia.

I said, 'Like me then.'

The place did seem empty without her. I was quite hoping this Frank might have to go away again and leave her, and Jimmy had left her biccies behind, so that was a good omen. Left the dog food too, but not my spare key.

A BLOOMIN' MIRACLE

Fruit Bowl pensioner Wilf Orme and friends are aiming to bring a bit of colour and greenery to a corner of their estate.

Not content with tending his allotment, Wilf, 75, applied to the council for help in creating a small garden between the Almond Blossom and Apple Bough towers.

The council have given the green-fingered seniors the go-ahead, but because of spending cuts there is no money available this year, so Wilf and his friends have decided to go it alone.

Retired factory foreman, Harold Ford, said, 'We've all chipped in with a few bob, and now we're all helping with the digging.'

Apple Bough tenant, Mike Jinks, said, 'I've no objections. I'd give them a hand, only I've got a bad disc.'

A resident of Almond Blossom who preferred not to be named said, 'I can't see it lasting five minutes, the vandalism we get round here.'

But Wilf and his pals are unde-terred. 'Hitler couldn't beat us,' he says, 'so we're not giving in to a few vandals. Plant a few trees, and then whatever happens you've left some-thing nice behind you.'

We were in Thursday's *Herald*, and they hadn't rubbed him out. It said, 'Pictured left to right, Blanche Fairbrother, Wilf Orme, Birdie Gibbs, Herbert Ford and a friend.' Only they'd mixed up Jimmy and Herbie. Wilf was waiting for me when I got back from Stratford, face on him like thunder, waving the paper.

'He had no business,' he said. 'Pushing in like that. He's nothing to do with it. I don't know what Herbie's going to say. I wouldn't be surprised if he doesn't ask for his garden money back.' Ridiculous thing to say. Herbie's not the type to fall out with people over a silly photo.

I said, 'It's only a newspaper. Come tomorrow morning it'll be in everybody's pedal bin.'

'Not in mine, it won't,' he said. 'I'm keeping a scrapbook of all this. I shall have to cut him out of it and join Herbie back on with sticky tape. I blame you. You should have told him to keep out of the picture. He's your husband.'

He is not.

I knew he'd been round, though, before I'd even got inside my front door. I could smell the surgical spirit. My memory's not bad, for an old coffin-dodger, but I'm better on smells than I am on what happened when and who said what. Clarice is disinfectant and talc. Olive is old gravy. Blanche is something out of the Avon catalogue. My brother Ted was plimsolls. My old dad was machine oil. And Jimmy's been Brylcreem and dog embrocation all the years I've known him.

I went in and there she was, standing in the kitchen, looking worried. No note, no key.

I said, 'Well, you weren't gone long.' But she wouldn't come to me. She just stood there shaking while I found her water bowl and a tin of rabbit chunks in jelly.

The rest of the afternoon I tried coaxing her, but she wouldn't move. She just stood there, looking at me. I put the telly on, lit the gas fire, and still she didn't want to know me, not even for half a Bounty bar.

Clark answered the phone. Blanche was at bingo. I said, 'You remember I was looking after Vanessa?'

'Yes,' he said. 'But the man fetched her home. Nan told me.'

I said, 'Well, he's brought her back again. Only she doesn't seem very happy. She won't even come and sit with me.'

He said, 'I could come round.'

He stayed with her in the kitchen for a long while, just sat on the floor and chatted to her about school and what he's doing in computers. I went and sat on my settee, poured myself a Guinness and left him to it. Jimmy always had more than his fair share of loopy dogs. Ones that wouldn't chase, head-turners, kennel-chewers, yappers, idiots that turned round in the trap. He had one when I was still with him, June Bug, used to get really worked up once they were at the track, specially if she could hear the hare. She'd sweat and dribble, and you could see the weight dropping off her. So he tried cotton wool in her ears and it worked a treat. She was a very smart trapper once she stopped dribbling herself to death. So then he moved her up a class, took her to run at Ramsgate and forgot to take the cotton wool out. Round comes the hare and June Bug hasn't heard a thing. Everything else is out of the traps like greased lightning, and she comes strolling out, wondering why everything's so quiet.

I said, 'How are you doing in there?'

He said, 'She's stopped trembling. I'm just telling her the story of Jairus's daughter, then I'll see if she'd like to come and sit with you.' He gets these stories from Sunday school.

In they came, after a bit, Clark coaxing her along. He said, 'Perhaps she'd like some chocolate?' I gave him some new bar with nuts in it. I'd only had a little bite and I didn't care for it. But she wasn't interested. Flakes were her favourite, but I didn't have any in. Clark had to finish it. He said, 'Perhaps she'd like some prawn cocktail-flavoured crisps?' But I wasn't going to let him go down to the Kabin on his own in the dark. Run into those Billies again and they'd soon turn his pockets inside out. Not just his pockets, come to think of it. He looked a bit disappointed.

I said, 'Are you peckish?'

'No thank you,' he said. Blanche has told him he mustn't come round expecting food. She's told him I've only got my pension, and it's not right eating my food when he gets good dinners at home. But I don't mind. What's a little bit of pork pie between friends?

So I did him a Snack-in-the-Box in the microwave, and when I came back in, there she was, lapping Guinness out of my glass like a proper lady.

He said, 'Mrs Gibbs? You know how Vanessa's got one ear that's brown and one ear that's a different colour brown? Well, they've got changed over. They're the other way round today.'

I put some more stout in a saucer for her and she finished the lot. I don't know what Dwyer's up to. As far as I know he always ran a decent outfit, kept everything legit. Not like Stan Motson. He was as bent as a nine-bob note. Jimmy was just straight up and down. But he's pocketed my key and now he's in and out of here with strange dogs like it's the PDSA. I don't think there even is a Frank.

I said, 'No wonder she wasn't answering to Vanessa. I suppose we'd better think of a different name for her then?'

He said, 'If I was allowed a dog I'd call it Goofer.'

He said, 'Do you think I'd better stay here tonight? Make sure she's not frightened?'

He said, 'I could fit on your settee, easy-peasy.'

I tried three times before Blanche answered. She sounded a bit downcast.

She'd been one number short of the jackpot. I said, 'I've borrowed Clark. He's been helping me with a dog of nervous disposition. Is he allowed to sleep here?'

She said, 'Oh, I don't know about that. He can't be late in the morning. He's having his eyes tested at ten to nine. He'll need a clean shirt.'

I promised he'd be up and home by eight o'clock. Then she phoned me back. She said, 'I forgot to tell you. Big Dwayne was going for a ride in a police van just as me and Olive came home. We got the taxi to slow down, and it was definitely him. Make it a quarter to, in the morning. He has to have a proper breakfast.'

I don't think it ever hurt anybody to have a bit of choccie for their breakfast once in a while.

I saw that Jen. She'd got a real shiner. Said she'd skidded on her bathroom floor and caught the edge of the sink, but that's what they always say. Caught somebody's fist, more like. Like that friend she lives with. A proper tough nut she looks, leather jacket and no eyebrows. Times I've passed her on the gangplank, or down at the Kabin fetching a paper, and she never speaks. I used to say good morning to her, but I stopped. I spend enough time talking to myself as it is. I wouldn't give her the time of day now, I wouldn't give her a gumboil now, not if I had a mouthful.

They're a funny pair. That Jen's all right; she's got some daft ideas, but she's nice enough. Brings me little odds and ends, funny things to eat. I always chuck them away as soon as she's gone, but at least she thinks of me. Blanche says they're a couple of lesbeens. They could be. She did say to me one time,

'I'm redefining my own sexuality, Birdie,' and I remember thinking, Uh-oh.

I was wearing the mauve tracksuit I got from the Mental shop. Only a fiver, and just the job for first thing in the morning, taking the Goofer out to spend her penny.

'Brilliant.' she said. 'When I am old I shall wear purple.' Winking at me. She's everlasting winking at me.

I said, 'When you're old you'll wear shoes that fasten with Velcro, same as the rest of us.'

Apparently Dwayne's back from helping the police with their inquiries. I don't know why they never manage to nobble him for anything. If you live round here it's as plain as day he's up to no good, but they never get him. He must have a charmed life. Anybody else, you forget to pay for your telly licence and you can end up in Holloway.

She said, 'I've been reading this marvellous book, Birdie, about goddesses and female monsters; about the days when women had real power.'

She's always talking about women being kept down. I don't know what she's on about. Nobody ever kept me down. Not unless I was willing.

She said, 'There were these creatures called the Lamia. They looked like women, except for their feet, and they lived in caves and mated with serpents.'

I said, 'Sounds like Dawn, next door to me.'

'Oh,' she said, 'you are a card.'

Aren't I just. It's the only thing to be once your skin's gone like crêpe paper and everything's moved south. Great big freckles on the back of your hands. You might as well be a card, because if you just stay quiet and nice and wear your poplin mac you blend in with the ruddy scenery. People pushing in ahead of you with their razor blades and their shower jelly when you've been standing there half the morning trying to pay for your cough sweets. You can either be a card or the invisible woman. It's up to you. Me, I'll carry on playing the London Palladium while I can. Sooner or later you breathe out and it's curtains. Sooner or later you do everything for the last time, including answering back. Including managing your own buttons. Get to my time of life and it's got to be sooner than later.

I said, 'You want to be careful on wet floors.'

Glad Wright went a purler in her kitchen, Valentine's Day, 1992. Next thing she was in the Co-op chapel of rest – broken hip and double pneumonia – her bits and pieces were all cleared out and her flat was let to Pakistanis. I've never seen anybody moved on so fast. A little spill of chip fat on your kitchen tiles and all your doilies and your china shepherdesses'll be down Mill Mead landfill faster than you can say 'knife'.

'I'm all right,' she said. 'I put arnica on it. I'm just off to my circle dancing. Dancing myself back to wholeness.'

Dancing herself to hugeness, more like.

Clarice has a girl come now to do her feet. All those years she should have been getting disability allowance, now she's lousy with money. When they told her she was entitled to back pay as well she said to me, 'I don't want all that, not when there's so many going hungry.' All those years she'd worked and she didn't like taking a bit out of the pot.

I said, 'There's nobody going hungry on your account. You should see the size of some of them queuing for their money at the post office. They're going to have to widen the door down there before much longer.'

So she took the back pay and she's been spending it. And I'm glad some of it's paying for the foot girl, because I hated cutting her big horny nails. I've never liked touching anybody else's feet.

I went over with her paper and her bread, and she

was sitting there listening to her hymns. That's another thing she's got now, tapes. 'The Day Thou Gavest Lord Is Ended' and all that jazz. Makes me feel like putting my head in the oven, but it takes all sorts. Course, you can't even do that these days. It's a different type of gas. For reasons of health and safety.

She said, 'Sit and have a cup of tea with me. I'm in a nicer mood now I've had my feet done.' Good thing too. I'd had a right old week with her. Reckoned I'd brought the wrong kind of milk. Then she said she'd asked for ham when I know for a fact she'd asked for corned beef. I couldn't do right for doing wrong.

She said, 'I've been thinking about when I was in Naples in 1943. We had some lovely sweet wine on Christmas Day. I don't know what it was called, because as you know I don't drink, but it was like nectar.'

Christmas of '43 I was down south, and some of us got invited to a social at Roedean. There was a crowd of soldiers billeted there, so we thought our luck was in, but they were all hospital cases, all been blinded and waiting to know the verdict. They couldn't dance and they didn't want to talk. Smokes, that's all they were interested in.

She said, 'And on Christmas Day Matron let us wear tinsel instead of our caps, and we had a sing-song. I never really enjoyed Christmas again after the war. Specially with the boys gone.'

Clarice had two brothers. Harry was shot down over Flushing, and the other one was in the Peace Pledge Union. He got excused the armed forces, but they sent him on an oil tanker and it took a direct hit. Every Christmas after that she volunteered to work, so the ones with families could get the time off.

I just went through to rinse the cups and put her shopping away. I wasn't gone more than two minutes. When I walked back in she was rummaging through her sideboard drawer. 'I know you've had it,' she said. 'You've been in here and taken my bank book.'

I went into Wilf instead of going straight home, I was so upset. He said, 'Pay no heed. She's just getting forgetful.' He said his old mum had gone the same way, saying things had been taken, accusing his Evelyn, and they always found the stuff stashed under her mattress. He said, 'It'll turn up, never fear. Mum used to swear we'd had cake and not given her any, and we'd find that under the mattress as well. She just didn't know she was doing it. And she'd say some very hurtful things to my Evelyn.'

I know that happens. But Clarice has never been hurtful to anybody. And then to do it to me. It was the way she'd turned on me like that, after all the years we've been friends, all the years I've been running errands for her. I couldn't help crying. It just came bubbling up from nowhere.

I begged him to go over and see if she was all right with him. She's always liked Wilf. Always used to be on at me to name the day.

He said he wouldn't go on his own, because a man has to be careful these days. Five minutes alone with a woman and you can be in the papers as a sex fiend. But he said he'd come with me to back me up. We went across about four.

'Oh,' she said. 'More visitors. I am having a busy day.' And she fetched out the photos of her leaving party, the day she retired. She knew the names of every face in that album, and I should know because I've seen it nearly as many times as she has. Wilf kept giving me the raised eyebrows, as if to say, Nothing wrong with *her*.

It wasn't till I got home and went in the bottom of my bag for my keys that I found it. I was glad it was safe, and I was sorry I'd been thinking bad thoughts about the girl who does her feet, but I didn't have a clue how it got in my bag. I thought I'd come clean. Put her mind at rest. So I dialled her number, heart in my mouth, and before I could tell her she said, 'Oh, Birdie, you're back. How are you, my dear? I've just had Harry and his wife sitting with me. We've been looking at photos and talking about the good old days.'

I took it over next morning. Put it in the fold of her newspaper and just slid it under the lace runner on the sideboard. She said, 'I've got Dr Das coming this morning to make sure everything's in working order. And I've got my pink undies on.'

I said, 'Do you want me to stay?' He's a lovely man, but you can't always catch what he says first time. Works all hours, and he's had his car broken into more times than I can count. The pond life, looking for pills. He ought to leave a few bottles of arsenic on his back shelf and do us all a favour.

'No,' she said. 'We'll be all right.'

I said, 'Well, just remember to keep those pink drawers on. You don't want some old beak telling you you were asking for it.' We laughed.

Sometimes, apparently, you can get a little bit of a blockage to the brain, like dirt in a fuel pipe, and then something bumps it clear, it floats away again and everything's back to normal. Olive read about it in her magazine.

The garden seat has walked. It lasted a fortnight, so I suppose we ought to phone the *Guinness Book of Records*, but Wilf's gutted. And of course nobody saw anything. It'd take two to carry it, and it's not the kind of thing Big Dwayne deals in. It'll be firewood somewhere by now.

There were half a dozen of those Billies hanging about when I went to catch the bus, one of them sitting in the gutter, the rest of them trying to get her to her feet, falling about, laughing and calling her name – Shannon.

I said, 'What's wrong with her?'

One of them said, 'Nothing, lady. She just buzzing her tits off.' And that set them all off laughing again.

I said, 'How come you're not in school?'

'Excluded,' she said. 'We too hot to handle.' It was Gemma, from along Wilf's landing. She's built like a Sherman tank.

Fifteen, they'd be. I was out of school when I was their age, washing sausage skins at Drummond's Pork Butchers, just till my dad could get me a start at the cardboard-box factory.

I said, 'You want to get yourself an education while you've got the chance. Best days of your life.' All the things they've got in schools now, trampolines and headphones and calculators. I'd be in there like a shot if they'd have me. And there they are, sitting in gutters, out of their heads on something.

'Naah,' she said, 'school's a waste of time. It's just reading and shit.'

I said, 'Did you see anybody stealing a garden seat from down between Almond and Apple?'

They said they hadn't. Just shrugged their shoulders.

I said, 'Where's Tamsin today?'

'Magistrates court.'

I said, 'What's she been up to?'

'Nothing. Going equipped.'

I said, 'Well, that's nice. She must be an inspiration to you all.'

Gemma said, 'Tamsin's got juice, lady. She's been inside.'

She has. And when they picked her up she shouted to the woman in Orange Grove who'd shopped her, 'I be up there, soon as I get out.'

Poor soul had to be rehoused, her nerves were so

bad, and Tamsin got three months at Bullwood Hall. Three months hard labour over a pool table, what I hear about these places.

I said to Wilf, 'We could put a card in Kareem's window. A reward for anybody who helps us get it back.'

'That's no use,' he said. 'They'll just pocket the dibs and then thieve the seat again.'

I said, 'How about setting it in concrete?'

'Not allowed,' he said. 'It's against regulations. You can't have kiddies falling and bumping their heads. At least they haven't touched the trees.'

Not yet.

Wilf said, 'What people round here need is work. A decent job for a decent wage, and then everything else'll follow.'

Everything's the Tories' fault, according to Wilf. Always going on about the bosses. Ask me, the unions are every bit as bad, crossing every t and dotting every i. One comrade to warm the pot, another one to open the tea caddy. They had all this at the bus depot, just after the war ended, because management had brought new timetables in without asking the unions. We'd just had Jerry dropping incendiaries on us, and they were out on strike, arguing about timetables.

He said, 'Things like this would never have happened in the old days. You could go out and leave your front door unlocked.' Listen to Wilf you'd think thieving was invented in 1946.

He said, 'You used to be able to trust your neighbours. Everybody getting along and helping each other out.'

I don't know that people were that much nicer while we had a war on. I remember a woman in Hope Street got sent a bit of tinned fruit from her sister in America, and nobody spoke to her for weeks.

I said, 'The only thing I can think is, on days when it's warm enough to sit down there we shall have to bring our own chairs down. Like those little folding seats you've got in your allotment shed. And we're not going to want to do much sitting now, are we? Too cold.'

'Yes,' he said, 'I suppose. It just destroys your faith in human nature. I think I'll let the *Herald* know what's happened. Give them a ring. They could take another picture of us, looking downcast, pointing to where the seat used to be. Might get us a new seat donated.'

He just wants another photo done, minus Jimmy Dwyer.

I told him about Tamsin being up in court and the Billie girl rolling around in the gutter.

He said, 'I dunno, Birdie. Things aren't what they used to be.'

Ask me, they never were.

KIDS GET SAY

A local truancy panel, set up by the National Union of Truancy Officers and the National Association of Social Workers, is inviting truants to pay them a visit and tell them why they think kids are staying away from school. With permission, as many of the interviews as possible will be recorded, and transcripts will be forwarded to the Government's Social Exclusion Think Tank, which aims to devise new ways of reducing truancy.

Kezia, 13, who gave evidence recently, said, 'I go home at dinner time because it's boring. Teachers should make it more interesting. I might stay more if we didn't have to copy things out of books.'

Grant, 11, says, 'It starts too early. I'd go if it was just in the afternoon. My mum agrees with me.'

Says Mo Johnson, chair of the local panel, 'We're not here to judge. These kids feel shut out from society. We have a duty to understand what they want and make education more relevant to their needs.'

That Jen came round again. I thought she said she'd brought me a bit of toffee. Little plastic tub she left on the side. I thought it was funny when she said about grilling it, but she is a weird one. Eats cauliflower without even cooking it. Anyway, when I had a look at it, after she'd gone, it wasn't like any toffee I'd ever seen. It looked like mattress foam to me, so it went straight in my pedal bin, pot and all.

She was telling me how bad-tempered her lady friend has been lately. The story is there's going to be people laid off where she works and she's not been sleeping well for worrying. When she gets tired she loses her rag; slightest little thing and there's saucepan lids flying. She was saying how she left her husband because he was a bad-tempered bastard and used to hit her, and she moved in with this Flick because women are different, and now it's déjà vu all over again.

I wouldn't live with a woman. Stockings dripping everywhere, and all that whispering. Do anything out of the ordinary – get a pay rise, or some extra clothing coupons – and they'd be whispering about you. They talk about women sticking together, but the only place they do that is at the bottom of the heap. All down there together, girls, never mind the weather, girls, carping about glass ceilings. But you start to do all right for yourself, then they don't like it.

I said, 'You could always live on your own, you know? There's a lot to be said for it.'

She said, 'I don't think I'm cut out for that. And Flick's all right. It's just a bad patch. How long did you stick it, living with Jimmy?' I can't remember things like that any more. Who can be bothered remembering things like that?

I said, 'Not long. Seemed like it at the time, though. Augie was the one I was with longest.'

'Oh,' she said, 'you've been married twice, then?'

So I told her the whole saga. How it was on and off between me and Jimmy and his poxy dogs for a while, and then Berto came along and Dwyer was history. That must have been about 1951 – I know sweets were still rationed. Berto was all right at the beginning. He had the finest head of hair I ever saw on a man. Beautiful black curls. It was his mother that was the problem. Didn't like him marrying an English girl, didn't like him not marrying a Catholic, told him he'd be dead of starvation if he waited for me to cook a proper dinner. She used to come round with a pair of white gloves and run her finger along everything, looking for dust. I never disappointed her on that score. Hit the jackpot every time. Piece of work she was. And I was stupid. Let her niggle me and started answering back. One night I told him it was time to ask his mother for his privates back and he hit me. Caught me on the chin. He wasn't much taller than me, but he packed a punch. I cracked a kitchen chair down on his head before I passed out, and it shattered. Cheap utility stuff. It was all you could get then. When I came to, a quarter of our chair ration was in pieces on the floor and he'd gone home to his mother. After that I gave country life a try.

There was a girl, Rene, I'd known in the service, moved to Norfolk and married a beet farmer. She said there was plenty of everything up there. Plenty of work, plenty of men, and I could stay with them for a bit, till I found my feet. Me and Norfolk never did click. There's nowhere safe to walk, for one thing. No pavements, no lights. Set foot on one of those lanes and you'd be mincemeat under a beet lorry. Nowhere to walk to anyway. Not even a little flea-pit. Rene had taken up crochet, and yet I remembered her when she used to sing round the clubs.

Close your eyes and you'd have thought it was Anne Shelton.

I managed three weeks at the sugar factory, which was two weeks and four days longer than I thought I'd last in a smell like that, and then I told Rene the time had come. I left some of my stuff there while I went across to the bright lights of Leicester and got myself some digs. By the time I went back to fetch my things she was expecting, and that was the last time I ever saw her. She had three boys, and then seven grandsons, and she never missed a Christmas card to me, didn't matter how many times I moved, until 1990. I suppose something happened.

I got a start at a place that made knitting machines, inspecting parts, and I worked Friday and Saturday nights in the Duke of Cumberland, for the company as much as the money. That was where I met Augie, which was a funny thing because he didn't drink. Didn't smoke, didn't swear, didn't run after women. He was wasted on me and that's a fact.

Augie's Aunty Cis had her name over the door of the Cumberland, and she ran the tightest ship I ever worked on. Nobody went home till everything was wiped off and polished, and that's how I got to know Augie, because he was a dab hand with a glass cloth. If things had worked out we might have had that place, when his Aunty Cis got too old to carry on. He could have done the books and I'd have run the show out front. She never really warmed to me, though. I worked hard. I've always been a grafter. I never was big on polishing round the house, but I was a diamond barmaid, and Cis wouldn't have argued that point. But I think she could see Augie was going to have his hands full. Anyway, hindsight costs nothing a pound.

We got married at a little church down the Belgrave Road. That was Augie's doing. He used to read his Bible every day. Never rammed it down my throat, though. We never had words over that, not until later anyway. Somebody said to me afterwards that the vicar shouldn't have allowed it, with it not being first time for me, but the fact is he didn't ask me. Ask me no questions, I'll tell you no lies.

We had two rooms over an ironmonger's. Augie was a Pru man, going door to door collecting insurance money, and I carried on at both of my jobs. We had the wireless on all day at the factory to stop you wanting to run screaming into the street. *Music While You Work, Workers' Playtime, Housewives' Choice*. Bent over that belt for hours on end, watching little machine parts roll past. It's a wonder I haven't got a hump on my back. Well, I do have a bit of a one, but show me an old lady that hasn't. If Augie had been making more I'd have packed the factory in and gone full-time at the pub.

I loved it – Friday night, Saturday night. We used to get a nice crowd in and we hardly ever had anybody turning nasty in drink. Of course, a barmaid has to listen to a lot of silly big talk, but you know nothing'll ever come of it. They're all big heroes after five pints of mild. A bit of advice from them and City need never have lost a match. And the size of some of those tench they nearly caught.

Augie used to come in from nine till closing time. And if there weren't glasses needed wiping he'd just sit in a corner with an orangeade, happy as a sandboy.

And that's how we tootled along. I've thought sometimes we might still have been together if that little baby hadn't come along and then died and caused so much trouble between us.

He never said he blamed me, not in so many words. To my mind she never was going to make it, weakly little thing. She never did have a good colour. And then, when the hospital said we should be prepared for the worst, that's when me and Augie started to have words. He wanted her christened. He wanted the chaplain fetched, get her done there and then, and we hadn't even agreed what we were going to call her. Five minutes, that's all we had, because they said she was at death's door.

Then she hung on for another fortnight after that, but it was like the wake had started without her,

Augie praying his prayers out loud all night long, and crying because I wouldn't join in.

We weren't there when she slipped away. You can't stay on Condition Red all the time. Life has to go on, so Augie was out on his rounds and I was at home, getting a bit of tea ready for when he came in. They told us when we went visiting, that night; took us into a little room and told us what we had to do to get the certificate and make the arrangements, and Augie asked to see her. I don't think it was usual, but they let him. I suppose they'd seen him with his prayer book. They knew he was a holy Joe.

The sister said to me, 'You're young. You'll get over it.'

Then we had to buy a burial plot in Gilroes Cemetery. He insisted we get one big enough for the three of us. All that palaver and we'd hardly known her five minutes. I had bags full of bootees and mittens she'd never even worn. After we'd buried her he said, 'There's room for the two of us in there with her, Birdie, but what if we have more kiddies?' But I knew that wasn't going to happen. The light had gone out in him, and he hated me going back to the Cumberland. He used to say, 'Maybe if you hadn't been doing two jobs. Maybe if you hadn't been on your feet so much behind that bar.'

Stan Motson had been drinking in the Cumberland

as long as I'd worked there. I wouldn't call him a regular, though. There wasn't anything regular about Stan. Cheeky face he had on him, and a great big Crombie overcoat full of hot goods. That town wasn't big enough to hold him, and that's how I ended up back where I'd started, just off the Barking Road, jumping every time there was a knock at the door.

Augie didn't stand in my way. He just got quieter and quieter after our sad loss, always reading psalms. And the day I started packing my bags he just went round to his Aunty Cis. I've wondered, over the years, if he ever met anyone else. I've wondered about that plot up at Gilroes as well, with room in it for two more. He could be lying in it already, him and some other Mrs Borders, stacked on top of that little baby. I could probably find out.

We had some great times, me and Stan. We got married at Finsbury Town Hall, with two window cleaners he fetched in off the street for witnesses, and we had a night in a top-dollar hotel up West. He used to take me dancing two or three nights a week, and he was always bringing things home for me: scent, stockings and watches, slightly damaged. I could never see anything wrong with them, but according to Stan they couldn't be sold. He brought me that many different ones I needed another pair of arms.

I went as a barmaid to a place in Canning Town, but I didn't like it. The Barrel, it was called. Barrel of vermin. There were women used to come into the snug, drank gin like it was tap water. Last time I was in that neighbourhood it'd all been knocked down and rebuilt, and it didn't look much better, either. Just a plasticated type of nasty, instead of plain ugly, and all different. I couldn't even get my bearings.

Anyway, the lady we were renting from said I had such nice neat writing I could get a job in an office, so I thought I'd give it a try. Much better money, and your shoes don't rot from paddling about in spilt ale. I didn't go short with Stan. He always put food on the table. One time we had so much tinned salmon stacked in the wardrobe I had to hang my blouses from the picture rail, but he never had the kind of job where you have to turn up every morning. He used to say, 'Nobody ever got to the Bahamas punching in.'

I did a month at the National Savings Bank and it seemed like a lifetime. You could hear a gnat breathe in that place. Then Sylvia that had the rooms downstairs from us said they were looking for somebody at her place. Mishkin's Furriers.

Old man Mishkin took one look at me and I was in. Nice cosy little office and you had permission to laugh any time you liked. Sylvia was over me, but that was all right. She did the telephone side of things and I did a bit of typing and the running up and down to the showroom and the cold store. I was always fast on stairs. Two at a time. And if Sylvia had gone to the lav I had to answer the phone, so I did get to talk to a few duchesses over the years. Lady Docker, we had. And Sabrina.

Fridays we had smoked salmon and we finished at three, and every year we got an extra day off for Yom Kipper. They were lovely to us at Mishkin's. Even after the old man retired and they went in for electric typewriters and adding machines, it was still the best place I ever worked. Out of business now, of course. It dropped off a lot after the Beatles and the Rolling Stones and all that crew, because nobody wanted to look nice any more. It was all denim jeans and leather jackets, even if you were in films.

Then they started having trouble with the balaclava brigade – animal rights. That was another thing that suddenly came in. There was a crowd of them started picketing, standing outside shouting 'Murderer' any time one of the duchesses came in, and then the shop got firebombed.

Me and Stan were all right. A bit like ships in the night sometimes, because just as I got home he'd be going out on a bit of business. But you can see too much of a body, and he never minded if I wanted to go dancing with Sylvia. There was talk of him carrying on with a barmaid from the Six Bells, but I never believed that. He was friendly with everybody. It was just his way. And I might have been with him yet, but it was a very terrible thing he did with that Christmas-club money. I'm not surprised he ran off, because there were people queuing to flay him alive, and as far as I know they never did get their money. I was finished with husbands after that. The only thing they did for me I couldn't do for myself was tap washers, and the water people'll do them for you free these days because of this global warming. That Jen said, 'Oh my goodness, Birdie, four husbands! And in those days as well, when divorce was so hard.'

I never bothered with divorce. Lining lawyers' pockets with good money. As it turned out, Stan ran to fat and had a seizure in the grandstand at Kempton Park in 1971, so it really would have been money wasted. And in a way that makes me a widow woman, but I didn't try getting a widow's pension, because according to the piece about it in the papers there was another Mrs Motson by then.

Berto I don't know about. He might still be with his mother, but that'd make her about 120. I wouldn't be surprised.

He said, 'Is this the Battersea Dogs' Home?'

I said, 'It's starting to smell like it. You'd better have a good story, Dwyer, in and out of my house with strange dogs.'

'What?' he said. Acting dumb.

I said, 'You must think I'm blind as well as stupid. Their ears weren't anywhere near the same. They didn't even watch the same telly programmes.'

'Oh,' he said, 'you noticed it wasn't Vanessa, then? I would have left you a little note, only I couldn't find a biro.'

He said her racing name was The Bouncer, but she answered to Freda and she'd had a bad case of track leg. He said they'd retired her and a nice family had taken her in, up Snaresbrook way, but they'd had to go away.

I said, 'Tenerife?'

'Funny enough, yes,' he said.

Funny enough, the bloke's name was Frank as well. Until later on. Then he turned into George. I thought he'd come to take her away, but he hadn't.

'Till next Friday?' he said. 'If you could see your way clear? Only I've got a bit of business to see to, and you know how it is? They don't like to be left long hours.'

I said, 'Are you getting paid for this? Babysitting dogs and leaving other people to do the dirty work?'

'Here,' he said, 'how about I take you out for a drink tonight, show my appreciation?'

'Bring some tins of dog meat in,' I said. 'Save me lugging them. That's the kind of appreciation I need.' If I had a quid for every time I climb those stairs in a week I'd be a happy woman. Up and down to Clarice, up and down tidying the garden, up and down with the Goofer. And the latest thing is Olive's hips are getting so bad I'm fetching shopping in for her as well. Great big cartons of milk and tinned golden syrup she wanted the other day, for a steamed pudding. She could have a sandwich and a Twirly-Whirly like me and save pulling my arms out of their sockets. Save my poor old legs. I can hardly move them first thing in the morning, ankles all seized up.

'Consider it done,' he said, 'and I'll pick you up about seven.'

Clark came up after school to see if I needed him to give the dog a run. I told him her name was Freda really. He said, 'Well, I think she's got used to Goofer.'

I said, 'Don't go getting attached to her. You know she's got to go back to Snaresbrook.'

He said he'd sit with her while I was out with Jimmy, in case she got lonely. Quarter to seven he was back on my doorstep with Blanche in tow. She won't go to bingo without Olive. Says it's not nice, a woman out at night on her own.

'I hear you've got a date tonight,' she said. 'I wondered if you'd like to borrow one of these little scarves? They finish a neckline off nicely.'

I've got scarves.

Twenty to eight when Jimmy showed up, and she'd managed to spin it out till then, telling me about the police paying Big Dwayne another visit and nothing coming of it again, and how he's suing them for harassment, looking for some big pay-out, and a load of stuff about Olive and the doctor and waiting lists that I'd heard a hundred times before, dragging it out so she could get a closer look at Jimmy.

I said, 'You didn't bring any dog food, then?'

He said, 'I *knew* there was something.'

Clark said, 'How long is Goofer going to be living here?'

'Hard to say,' Jimmy said. 'But I hear you've been

helping out with her, like a good boy, taking her for walks, you and your mum?'

Blanche had never taken her for any walk.

Clark said, 'This is my nan, not my mum.'

'Never,' he said. 'You're never old enough to be this young man's nan.' Course, that started her simpering. He said, 'You must have been a child bride, that's all I can say. Are you coming with us? Have a few drinks?' I don't know what men see in her. Great big backside on her.

'No,' she said, 'you and Birdie don't want me playing gooseberry.'

'Don't be so daft,' he said. 'Pair of old-timers like us. We'd run out of things to say before you were even born. Go and fetch your coat.'

And Clark said, 'Yes, go on Nan. You hardly ever go out now Mrs Rankin's poorly.' I tried giving him my beady eye, but he didn't get it. Wouldn't occur to him I might like to be treated to a night out without Blanche queering my pitch, smelling of that body spray of hers.

She said, 'Well, how about we give Wilf a call? See if he fancies a pint? Then we'd be a nice even number. What do you think, Birdie?'

I said, 'Yes. And how about the Treorchy Male Voice Choir? See if they're at a loose end as well.' Nobody considers you when you're an old woman.

They don't think you might like a bit of a night out, a nice cosy drink with your husband.

So then we had to wait around in the cold outside Orange Grove while Blanche coaxed Wilf, and then when he'd said, 'All right, just a quick one,' hanging around while he was tidying away his gardening books, checking he hadn't left the oven on, ironing his antimacassars, I shouldn't be surprised.

We went to a place called Blimey O'Reilly's, music so loud you had to shout. Wilf sat there nursing a ginger beer, looked like he'd lost a shilling and found a tanner. He only perked up when Blanche asked Jimmy if he'd met me in the service. Jimmy just said no and started talking about the dogs, but Wilf said, 'Which outfit were you with, then?' Wilf knew perfectly well about Jimmy's feet, because I remember telling him.

I said, 'Reserved occupation,' and Wilf said, 'Right. One of them.' There was no need for that. Jimmy'd have done his bit if they'd have had him. And Blanche didn't have to have another shandy, Jimmy explaining the difference between Sumner hares and McGee hares, shouting in her ear and her pretending to be interested. And I couldn't have talked to Wilf, even if he hadn't been in a sulk, because as far as I know he can't lip-read. I hope all these kids are learning, though, because they're all going to be deaf by the time they're thirty.

Snake Eye had been gone, must have been nearly three weeks. I was just thinking of putting the flags out and he came back. First way I knew was his stereo was making the windows rattle. Then the door-slamming started. That boy couldn't close a door quietly if you paid him.

Olive says he's the way he is because he's never had a man around to keep him in line, but I don't think it's that simple. Her Brian had a dad – worked down the Albert Docks all his life, went to chapel every Sunday – and look what an idle toe-rag he's turned out to be.

Same with my brother, Ted. We were brought up to know right from wrong, and if it slipped our minds we soon got a reminder from our dad's belt, but Ted still went off the straight and narrow.

They evacuated him to Norfolk the first month of

the war, but he was soon back. He didn't like the woman he'd been billeted with. She'd kept washing his hair with Derbac soap because he was lousy. We all were. Nits, fleas, threadworms. We never needed to feel lonely, all the wildlife we had on us in those days. Bedbugs as well. They used to live behind the wallpaper, and you'd never know they were there till you were tucked up in bed. Then they'd come out.

Anyway, this evacuation lady didn't like the way Ted had been dragged up, and she clipped his ear for starting on the bread and butter before they'd said grace, so he did a runner. But by the time he got home they'd shut the school, so that was his education finished. When they started rounding up the Italians and they came for the Rizzi brothers, he stood on the corner of our street and shouted, 'Filthy Boche'. Ted never was the sharpest tool in the box when it came to geography.

He was fly, though. He went into the salvage business, liberating stuff from houses that had been bombed out. He got a birching the only time he was caught. The beak said if he'd been older he'd have been put away, and if he ever got caught again he'd be hanged, with there being a war on and everything, but as it turned out he fell down a coal cellar in the blackout and broke his neck. He'd have been sixty-eight now.

Broke his neck and broke our mum's heart, but she'd never have a word said against him. We only had one picture of him and she kept it on the mantelpiece, where she could talk to it. 'I was just telling our scamp,' she used to say. And that's how Dawn is with Snake Eye.

I passed him on the stairs. Slithered past me with his stupid skateboard. I said, 'It'd be nice if you'd turn that bongo music down without me having to fetch the environment people again.' He gave me the finger, as per, so I went round to see Dawn.

I said, 'I'm not having it. I pay my rent and I'm entitled to quiet enjoyment.'

She said, 'Nobody else has said anything.'

That's because they're deaf as posts already. Most of them are as bad as he is. They're not happy with that racket they play until it makes the furniture move.

She said, 'Oh, don't go complaining, Birdie, upsetting him. I don't want him disappearing again. He's only just come back.'

I said, 'Well show him where the quieten-down knob is. Where's he been anyway?'

'He had a bit of trouble,' she said, 'with Big Dwayne. He's been lying low. But he's come back with a terrible cough.'

He did look bad, I must say. Nails all chewed. Eyes like a bloodhound. He has a zed bed in the lounge because Dawn's flat is only one bedroom, same as mine, and she sits there watching her morning telly programmes with the sound turned down until he shakes a leg. Sour socks, that's what her lounge smells of. And other things.

The trouble with Dawn is she's been on those tablets so long she hardly knows what day of the week it is. Unless it's sign-on day. They never miss that. Ordinary days, though, there's nothing much doing round there till dinner time. Curtains shut tight, doesn't matter if we're having a heatwave, a tropical heatwave. But once they're up and moving you know about it. Doors banging, people in and out, and they all look like they could do with a good hose down.

Dawn has half of Plaistow knocking at her door, and one time they got it wrong and came to mine. Two boys in stupid hats and baggy trousers, standing there like real hard men.

I said, 'What do you want?'

'Product,' they said. 'We just be looking for product.'

Product. That'll be something bad, whatever it is. And you can never find a policeman when you want one.

Blanche says he's dealing in Rits; she's nearly certain. They get it on prescription for this attention deficit syndrome, which means they can't sit still for two minutes and learn their long division. It's all the rage round here. There's hardly a kid on this estate hasn't got it.

So they fetch their Ritalin from the chemist, trade it in with Mr Big next door to me, and then he sells it on to some other sad cases. Stops you wanting to eat, apparently.

I said to Dawn, 'I see he's still not working.'

'He's not well enough to work,' she said. 'He's got yuppie flu. I don't suppose you could lend me a couple of quid for the electric meter? Just till tomorrow?'

I told her I couldn't spare it. I'd got Clarice's purse on me, with her little bit of change, so I showed her that. Just little brown coins, wouldn't even buy you a box of matches.

'Oh dear,' she said, 'I shall be sitting with candles tonight and no telly.'

I tried not to look too pleased. I was thinking it'd be no bad thing for Dawn's electric meter to be empty. I was thinking I might get a night's peace, without his moron music. As long as he hadn't got batteries for his bongo machine. As long as he didn't come home out of his skull on something, knock her candles over and cremate us all in our beds.

I said, 'Can't he get a place of his own?'

She said, 'He's all right here. You're the only one that's against him.'

Which definitely isn't right, because when he had that old Vauxhall and he used to drive round the Fruit Bowl like it was Brands Hatch, there were some of them getting up a posse to lynch him, specially the ones with young kiddies. And then, there's always some aggravation going on between him and Big Dwayne. They ought to put them in a circus ring together. Do the tax-payers a favour and let them finish each other off. They could sell tickets for it. Put the takings in the blind box or something. I'd go. Front row, I'd pay for.

Blanche came by later, with some magazines for Clarice.

She said, 'You'd think he was giving money away next door to you. I've just seen three girls going in and three more coming out.'

I said, 'Well, I don't think it's his body they're after, that tidemark he's got round his neck.'

I don't know, though. If it's the girls I think she means, they don't look too fresh and dainty themselves. It's a wonder to me those Vosene people haven't gone out of business.

Clark said, 'Will you come to Harvest Thanksgiving at my Sunday school?'

I said, 'Can't your nan go?'

'Oh,' he said, 'she's coming anyway. But I want you to come and be my other nan.'

I said, 'What about Mrs Rankin?'

'No,' he said, 'she's got a bone in her leg. Why don't you want to come?'

I couldn't really say. I just didn't. I said, 'It's been a long time since I was in a church. I've forgotten all the words.'

'That's all right,' he said. 'I'll show you where it is in the book. And afterwards you can buy something. Everybody takes something, like a cabbage, and everybody buys something, and the money goes for the starving babies in Africa.'

I said, 'I don't buy cabbage. Ask your Aunty Olive

again. It sounds right up her street.'

'No,' he said, and I could see his little eyes filling up. 'She's not my other nan. You don't have to buy a cabbage.'

I said I'd think about it.

I saw Blanche down at the bins later. 'Yes,' she said, 'just bring anything. Bring a tin of beans. We'll see you on our landing, about half past ten, and don't be late whatever you do, because Clark'll be laying eggs.'

So Saturday night I put my hair in rollers and cleared all that Jen stuff into a carrier bag: something that's supposed to look like meat and taste like meat but isn't, and some green Jap stuff that smells like low tide on a hot day, and chromium tablets that had never been opened. And there were two sachets of Angel Whip – I think they must have been free with something. They went in the bag, and a box of Grape Nuts. I don't know where half the things in my cupboards sprang from. Get rid of the cupboards, that's what I think. Rip them all out and just keep your cup and saucer on the draining board. Otherwise, as soon as you've got cupboards and drawers, stuff comes creeping into them. Pickle forks and cake stands and packets of parsley-sauce mix. Sometimes I think I've wandered into the wrong flat.

I told Clarice where I was going. 'Oh, how lovely,' she said. 'When we were children we used to take the fruit round to the poor and the elderly.'

I said, 'That's us now, Clarice. But this stuff's for Africa.'

'Quite right, too,' she said. 'We've got more than enough to spare.'

She has. Now she's getting all these allowances she's sitting up there like Lady Rothschild, wondering what to spend it on next.

I'd already done her shopping. I was only phoning her to see if she'd had any more trouble with the Billies. They'd been shouting through her letter box. Pushed something through it once as well. A disgusting thing I had to pick up with her coal tongs and drop in her pedal bin. I was just glad Clarice didn't know what it was. You don't want to have to find out about that kind of thing when you're her age. I swear they've got things in the zoo better behaved than those Billies.

'I've had a lovely day,' she said. 'The Indian lady from along the landing brought me some coconut sweets, and there was a nice film on this afternoon with Grace Kelly. And a man came to the door to see if I wanted my roof checking.'

I said, 'You didn't give him money, did you?'

'No,' she said, 'I told him I didn't keep money here, so he'd have to come back, but he couldn't. He said it was a special offer just for today.'

I said, 'You haven't got a roof, Clarice. There's four

floors on top of you, and anyway, the roof's up to the council.'

'I know that,' she said. 'And I don't have a damp patch anywhere. I'd have noticed if I'd got rain coming through.'

I said, 'Promise me you won't have any workmen in. Not even if they say they're from the council. They're supposed to write and tell you. And don't you ever give money to men that come to the door.'

'I won't,' she said. 'I'm not a fool. I already promised the Indian lady. She brought me some sweets round. And Birdie did my shopping. Apparently she's going to a harvest supper with her little boy. We used to have harvest suppers when I was a girl.'

Blanche says she shouldn't be on her own. I don't know. I think she'd be worse if we got her moved out and she had to get used to a whole new place. Wheelchairs all in a circle, like wagon trains, and the telly never turned off. She may forget who's who and who she's told what, but at least she knows our faces. At least she doesn't get strangers asking her about her bowels.

I went down to Blanche's landing in good time. Olive's boy, Brian, was just coming up the stairs, puffing and panting. I said, 'Are those lifts out again?'

'No,' he said, 'it's me. Can't use them. I've got anxiety.'

I said, 'I thought it was your back.'

'Oh, it is,' he said, 'I've got a corset. Day at a time, that's how I take it, day at a time.' Him and his lady friend were taking Olive for a drive out.

Clark looked like he'd been polished, and he'd got a basket of veg nearly as big as himself. 'Look,' he said, 'I've got parsnips and everything. And my nan's got a marrow, but it's too big to fit in here.'

When we got to St Matthew's Clark said he'd take my carrier bag. Bold as brass, he went up to the altar rail with our stuff. Everybody there seemed to know him. Funny, I worry about him when I see him at home because he's such a skinny little strip. He won't say boo to a goose, and you've got to, living where we do, but in that church he looked grand. Really grown up. I could see him having the makings of a vicar a few years down the line. He brought the chromium tablets back, though. He said, 'I don't think these are harvest, Mrs Gibbs.' I stuck them in my pocket. He was probably right. It'd be more like mining than harvesting.

We had a good old singalong. 'We Plough' and 'Let Us With A Gladsome'. Me and Blanche had both forgotten our reading glasses, but the words come back to you somehow. I tried to get the little cushion off its hook when they started praying, but Clark whispered that old people weren't expected to kneel down. Then the vicar gave a long talk about a hole in the sky over the South Pole. Blanche nodded off and I nearly joined her. Then just before the end, who should come sneaking in but Wilf Orme in his best sports jàcket, probably come to make sure his marrow went for a good price. Clark's face lit up like a 100-watt bulb. 'Hello, Uncle Wilf,' he said. 'My veggie basket's definitely the best. I'm the only one that's brought parsnips.' So, it's *Uncle* Wilf now.

I'd been out all morning. I came from the bus, called in the Kabin for some choccie, and then as soon as I turned the corner by Cherry Tree I could see something was happening. There were half a dozen of them standing there, looking up at our tower, and I could see something moving about on the roof.

That big Samantha with the brown baby was standing with them. She said somebody ought to fetch the police, but the phone box was wrecked. I said, 'Is it kids up there?'

'No,' she said, 'it's Snake Eye. He keeps coming to the edge and then going back. I reckon he's necked something.'

My eyes are good, apart from reading, but I couldn't be sure who it was up there. Then some women from Orange Grove came out on their landing, about level three, and started looking. I tried shouting up to them, but they couldn't hear me. Everybody kept saying someone should go up there, see what his game was, but nobody was willing to budge, in case they missed something. Then he came to the edge again, closer to the edge than I liked the look of, and I could see it was him.

I said I thought I'd go and phone the police. That Samantha said, 'Yeah. And phone the telly people as well. Get them round.'

Our lift was working. There was a little pile of something reeking in the corner – I didn't look too closely; I just held my breath and got out at seven. I thought I'd try Dawn first, but her door was wide open and nobody in. Just her electric Rudolf's red nose winking away in her window. I put my bags inside my door and went back to the lifts. I could see over the walkway railing that there were more of them down there already, just standing watching. I called down the stairwell, in case there was anyone about, and that Jinks peered up at me.

I said, 'Dial 999. Tell them we've got Snake Eye on the roof, looks like he might jump.'

'Can't help you there,' he said. 'Been cut off.'

I said, 'Well, bang on some doors and get somebody else to do it.'

'All right, all right,' he said. 'No need to shout.'

I took the lift up to ten. That's as far as it goes.

After that there's just a few steps, and two doors you're not supposed to go through – one for all the lift gear and one to the outside. They were both swinging in the breeze.

I'd never been out on the roof before. It was nice up there, sun shining, lovely and quiet, and a bit of frost still lying. The door brings you out facing across to Cherry Tree, so I thought he'd be straight in front of me, but there was no sign of him. Then I heard Dawn.

There's a hut up there, in the middle, says high voltage on it, and they were round the other side of that. Snake Eye was standing up, but safe enough, and Dawn was on her hands and knees, crying.

'Kevin,' she kept saying. 'Come home. It'll be all right.' He didn't move, but it was like he was lost, like he was listening to something, and then a bit of breeze got up and made the door bang, and he saw me. He started shaking his head and backing away, nearly to the edge, and his skateboard tucked under his arm, like he was going out to play. Dawn was shouting, 'No, Kevin!' and waving at me to get away from them. I only meant to help.

I stayed out of sight, but I could still hear them. He was talking to himself, and Dawn kept saying, 'There's nobody there, Kevin, only Birdie. There's nobody after you.'

I edged round the other side of the generator, just enough so I could see him, and I was concentrating that hard on not making a noise I didn't notice the pigeons. They went up in the air in one big flutter, straight at him.

There's a little low wall runs all the way round the roof, with concrete coping on the top. 'Oh no,' he said, and he stepped up onto it, like ten floors up was nothing.

Dawn was screaming, 'Birdie, help me get him down.' But I couldn't look, he was so near the edge.

I heard a siren. I thought, if they were on their way, we only needed to keep him talking for a little bit longer. They'd come and talk him down — special trained people — and they'd have nets down below, in case he did go over. But it didn't get any nearer. I think it was an ambulance going across to Whipp's Cross.

I moved round slowly, till I was nearer Dawn. I said, 'Come and help me with your mam, Kevin. Look what a bad way she's in.' He was quiet for a bit.

I said, 'Your mam needs you to come and look after her. Get her home and make her a cup of tea.' I could see he was thinking about it. Dawn was hanging on to me with one hand, and reaching out with the other one, trying to coax him. I didn't know what to do. People go on courses for things like that. I said, 'How about a piece of chocolate?' It was all I'd got on me.

I fetched it out slowly and broke a square off, and blow me if he didn't step down off the ledge and take it from me. It was melting a bit, from being in my pocket. He took it from me and put it in his mouth, and I thought, That's the ticket!

I said, 'I've got a bit more, if you'd like it.' First time I'd ever spoken to him without getting a load of lip back.

I said, 'How about finishing this chocolate and then taking your mam home?'

Then he lay down along the coping, with his knees tucked up and his arms round his skateboard, like a little lad going to sleep.

'It's too high, Mam,' he said, and then he rolled over the edge, just like that. It was all quiet and sunny up there, as if everything had stopped still. My legs had gone to water. And then Dawn went down on her knees, holding her arms out where he'd gone over, gurgling his name, just gurgling it, not loud at all.

I don't know how long we were there. It seemed like a long time. I stayed with my arm round her till somebody came. I don't think she knew, but I didn't dare leave her. I didn't want her going over there after him.

When you've seen a terrible thing, you just keep seeing it, over and over in your mind's eye, like your brain's trying to sort it out. Like your brain's saying, No, that can't be right. Try again.

We were called out once to a factory that had been hit in Frewin Street. There were two officers with hoses up on the turntable, and things seemed to be dying down. I was parked just back from them, talking to one of our drivers, and then, all of a sudden, flames came shooting out again, from down below, and the factory walls went – crumpled, just as if they were made of paper – and the men were gone. They found their helmets later on. When I got back to the station, apparently I got a rollicking because the paint down one side of my bike was blistered from the heat, but I don't remember anything about that. I just kept seeing those men again, there one minute, then gone. And Snake Eye, taking a piece of choccie, then gone.

The door banged again, and a WPC popped her head round and saw the pair of us. Her radio crackled. I couldn't make it out, but I did hear her say she could use a doctor upstairs, if he wasn't needed down below.

It was that darkie doctor that Clarice has. Dr Das. Always wears a mustard-coloured pullover, whatever the weather. Dawn couldn't walk. They fetched a wheelchair up from the ambulance, and that's how we got her back down to seven. I don't know how I got there. I could have used a ride in a chair myself. Patti came out and said we could take her into her place. She was another one with a winking Rudolf. Tree all trimmed up and a baby Jesus scene, with fairy lights all round it, and it was only the beginning of December.

'Hot sweet tea,' Dr Das said. He said she was suffering from shock and mustn't be left. He said her family should be sent for, but the only family I knew of had just rolled over the edge of Apple Bough.

ROOF MAN NAMED

The man who died after police were called to an incident on the roof of a tower block on the Fruit Bowl Estate has been named as Kevin Arlo Banks, aged 27.

A former pupil of Aldersbrook Comprehensive School, Mr Banks was single and lived with his mother in the Apple Bough tower, where the tragedy occurred.

Police have been questioning residents about events leading up to the fatal fall, but foul play is not suspected.

A neighbour of the Banks family, Miss Bridie Gibbs, was praised for her attempts at persuading Mr Banks to leave the roof area.

Crystal therapist Ms Jen Marsh, one of several witnesses, said, 'She's a totally amazing woman, going up on the roof at her time of life. I blame the council, though. People shouldn't be able to get out onto dangerous roof areas and have tragedies.'

A spokesman for the Borough Council said, 'Repeated vandalism has made it impossible for us to prevent access to roof areas and lift shafts. We shall, of course, be looking to see if lessons can be learned from this, but budgetary restrictions make any immediate changes unlikely.'

A 24-hour Freefone counselling service is available to any witnesses or associates of Mr Banks who may be suffering from post-traumatic stress.

An inquest will open on December 7th.

———————————————————

Olive said, 'Well, look at it this way, Birdie, he won't be troubling you any more, playing his stereo all night.' What kind of a thing was that to say? I mean, he was a scrounging, thieving piece of scumbag vermin, but I never wanted to see him going off any roof, going off in front of his mam like that. And just when he'd had a piece of chocolate and we thought we were home and dry.

I just wonder if things would have turned out different if I hadn't gone up there. Say I'd just phoned the police and left Dawn on her own up there with him. And then, it might have been the chocolate. If he'd taken pills, which he definitely had, because they did tests to prove it, maybe something in them didn't agree with the chocolate and just tipped him over. Olive's Brian's lady friend was on something a while back, and she couldn't eat Marmite.

Clarice said, 'He's at peace in the arms of Jesus.' But we don't know that for certain. Clarice doesn't really know what he was like. And she gets mixed up. She can tell you all about when she was a girl, and the war, but if you bring her a different brand of evaporated milk, say, if it's on special offer, she says you're trying to cheat her out of money.

She's being assessed. They send somebody round to see if you know who the prime minister is. Who cares? And if they want to know about Clarice, they should ask me. I'm the one that sees her every day, and she remembers all her history and her kings and queens of England. She doesn't always know whether she's had her breakfast, but she knows the Gunpowder Plot was 1605. It's like patchy fog. Even when you're out of it, even when her mind's as clear as crystal, you have to mind how you go with her, because you never know what she'll be like just down the road. She read all about Snake Eye in the paper, but sometimes she asks me, 'How's that little boy going on, that fell off your tower?'

Dawn says everybody let him down. She says nobody ever gave him a chance. She wasn't getting at me in particular. I suppose she remembers it was me up there with her when it happened, but she's never mentioned it. Just keeps talking about when he was a little boy, holding her hand on the way to school.

Showing everybody her photos. I couldn't look at them. I pretended, but I wasn't really looking. I'm not one for photos. Cleared all mine out years ago. I've just got Clark's school photo and I didn't really want that, but they have a new one taken every year and he does like me to have one.

I haven't been sleeping too well. That PC Lines came to see me, said I'm entitled to counselling, but I told him not to bother. I haven't got time to be staying in, waiting on some trick cyclist. I wake up about three, and that's me done for the night. I keep thinking about him, wondering what it was all about. He never went anywhere, apart from Glen Parva Young Offenders and a couple of proper nicks. He never did anything. Slept all day, sponged off his mum, thieved off his neighbours. Same old jeans on every day and a silly ring through his eyebrow. I might not have much — I haven't got a flat full of fancy cushion covers and fridge magnets, like Olive — but at least I've been about a bit. I've seen life.

I was getting seven shillings a week at the cardboard-box factory, and after Spain got bombed we thought we'd be next, so we went on a first-aid course, down the Civil Defence, me and my dad. First night we went they did snake bites, so I never bothered going back for the second one. I went to a jitterbug marathon at the Paramount instead.

Then I heard they were recruiting girls for the fire brigade, and I was down there like a shot. Two nights a week, learning how to do the phones. It wasn't much, but I thought if ever anything serious started they might be glad of us to go out on the appliances. I couldn't wait.

Course, nothing happened. We'd just sit there, playing whist or knitting, and there was no sign of any Germans, even after war broke out. I was on the switchboard at West Ham station and one night this message came, they were looking for volunteers to be despatch riders, full-time. Our station officer said, 'They'll never take you,' because I was only five feet one, but they did. They put me on a 250cc at New Cross Speedway, and I passed with flying colours. Was I glad to see the back of that cardboard-box place. I got some leather leggings, Navy issue, and boots and gauntlets, and I was ready for Hitler. Ready for anything. After that they used to send me out all over the place, testing the street alarms. I think they were hoping I'd get lost, because they didn't really have anything much for us to do. Till one Sunday teatime.

I'd just gone on watch and we got a Condition Purple. Next thing we knew, Beckton Gas Works was in flames and they were swarming over, hammering the docks, our side of the river and down Woolwich side as well. There were calls coming in and we hadn't got anything left to send out. There wasn't a pump left in the station.

It did ease off for a bit and they sounded the All Clear, but those devils were soon back. Then the power went off and the phones, and after that we didn't stop all night. Me and two other riders, Min and Ivy, we were back and forth between the pumps and Lambeth Control, running messages. We didn't have any trouble with the blackout that night; the sky was lit up like high noon. Best night of my life that was.

We were stood down at seven the next morning, and I could no more have slept than fly. I had a quick wash down and a gallon of tea, and I could have taken the Luftwaffe on, single-handed. There was an old boy across the street from us, used to reckon we were a waste of petrol, but he changed his tune after that night.

Things were never as good after they nationalized us. All we'd done in the Blitz, and they couldn't leave well alone. I blame Herbert Morrison. They stood a lot of us down because of all the new girls coming in. Said we'd earned a rest. But it was boring. It was all mending hoses and doing keep fit. Sitting at a table fitting little bits together for Mosquitoes till I thought I'd scream. I wanted to get back on my motorbike.

I was glad when things hotted up again and they

asked for volunteers to transfer down south. That was when I met Jimmy. And I didn't get back to London till the V2s started. I didn't sleep well then, either. You could hear them coming, like a train, and I used to think, I've come this far. Be just my luck to cop one now.

That Jen says the whole estate is full of people who feel like doing what Snake Eye did. She says we've got very bad *feng shui*. Everything's *feng shui* with her these days. She wanted me to move my bed. I said, 'All right, I'll have it on a beach in St Tropez.' And she keeps on about my front door, because it sticks.

'Oh, Birdie,' she says, 'that's not propitious.' But it's only the damp. Ugly buildings make ugly lives, she says. But the way I look at it, you can slap a bit of wallpaper up and make them nice enough inside. Every other year I do my walls. And we made our little garden.

That's another thing that's been keeping me awake. Someone from Cherry Tree has got a petition up. They want it to be called the Kevin Banks Memorial Garden. They want the council to pay for a plaque. Wilf says over his dead body, and I'm with him all the way. Then I suppose they'd have to call it the Wilf Orme and Birdie Gibbs Memorial Garden.

I've been thinking I might give it another try with Jimmy. He's got his place near Brighton, and he's said I'm welcome to go and stay. Any time, he said. I wouldn't put up with any funny business, but he knows that. We'd just be a bit of company for each other, instead of talking to the telly. And two pensions have got to be better than one. We could even get a little dog.

I don't like going along Blackberry Hedge any more. There's been two pensioners had their bags snatched coming down there and they say they're probably no older than ten, the boys that did it. And I've had somebody looking in my window. I went into the kitchen Monday night, just to fetch another Guinness for me and the Goofer while the adverts were on. I didn't bother with the light. And there was this boy looking in at me – thin, ugly face on him and a woolly hat, just standing there, staring in. I don't know how long he'd been there. He might have been looking for my microwave. Videos and microwaves are their favourites. Nice and easy to lift. I shouted the Goofer to come, but she's no guard dog. And the thing I didn't like was he wasn't bothered I'd seen him. He didn't run off. He just stood there, staring at me. And then he smiled. That was the worst bit. I'd got my chain across, and my bolt. I knew he couldn't get in. But it's given me the heebie-jeebies, thinking he might have been watching me before, and the front of him, just standing there, smiling at me. Ask me, he didn't look all there. Wilf says it's because of Care in the Community.

So now I've got the microwave in my living room, and I bring everything through about four o'clock – bottles, choccie supplies, crisps for the Goofer – so I don't have to go in the kitchen after dark. I might put broken glass on my window sill as well, just in case he tries anything. It's getting like the siege of ruddy Mafeking, living round here. And I've got empty flats either side of me. Dawn's gone to her sister's in Romford, and Patti's on remand for stolen credit cards.

Then it looks like I shall be losing Clarice. She'd put a mousetrap in her drawer, because she's convinced everyone's after her money, so her helper got a nasty shock. Came to get her dressed one morning, went to the drawer to get her a clean vest and the trap snapped shut on her. All that happened was her fingernail turned black and fell off, but she reported it to the office, so that was another question mark against Clarice's name, and of course she's got no family to speak up for her. I could. I could say there's enough of us to keep an eye on her, but I don't know that it's the right thing to do.

Some people like it in these nursing homes. Olive can't wait till it's her turn. Anyway, it's probably too late for Clarice, because she had to be assessed again, after the business with the mousetrap, and they must have caught her when she was having a funny five minutes, because they put her straight on the top-priority list for Lime Trees. That'll be a one-way ticket. The only way you ever come out of Lime Trees is in the back of a long black motor.

I don't know what I shall do when I haven't got Clarice to look after. She's not as nice as she used to be, nor as sharp, but you still get more sense out of her than Olive, Blanche and Nellie from the chemist's all stacked up together. A highly educated woman, Clarice. Didn't finish school till she was nearly seventeen.

She was in the Territorials, and she started off on the ambulance trains, running injured men from the clearing, stations across to Dieppe. She was on one of those runs, just before Dunkirk, and they had to bale out because the track was blown up. It was every man for himself, and there wasn't room for her to ride in any of the trucks that picked them up. So she borrowed a bike from the back of somebody's house. It took her nearly a week to get to Cherbourg, and nothing to eat but a bit of that French bread and raw onions. Sleeping out. If the Germans had caught her she'd have been shot. Then they shipped her home, and her dad said she was to stay put, told her she'd done her bit, but when they asked her to go to Suez she thought it'd be nice to see a bit more of the world.

Mozzies everywhere, she told me, and rats. Mind you, I've seen rats here, round the bins and the garages, and somebody won a prize for building this eyesore. I wonder if he's ever been back to see it? I wonder if he still sleeps well at night?

But according to Clarice the rats out there had the cheek of the devil, and if a man had got his leg in a cast, they'd come right up to him, just stroll up and nibble on the plaster. She told me she always carried a big stick with her, wherever she went. And not just in case of rats, either.

She was out there for El Alamein. And there was an Australian soldier she was keen on, had been wounded at Benghazi. They patched him up, though, and he was recalled, and that was the last she ever saw of him. She only ever mentioned him the once, one Christmas, when we'd put a dent in a bottle of cherry brandy. Strict abstainer, Clarice. She thought it was cherryade. She said she'd never looked at another man after she lost her Aussie. She said it had never bothered her, not having sex. Said her mother had had it, and she reckoned she'd rather play bridge any day.

She was on a hospital carrier after that, in Italy, going right in to shore to pick up wounded men. They'd been loading casualties from Anzio, and they were ordered to stand out to sea for the night, because of the shelling. Sitting ducks, they were, all lit up like Blackpool Illuminations, and they took a direct hit. They had to abandon ship, and there were men in the water only just been operated on. She's never told me the details, but I think that's why she got her gong. I did ask her what happened, but she wasn't letting on, not even after all those cherry brandies.

And if me and Jimmy got back together, I wouldn't have any more of this rigmarole at Christmas – Blanche inviting me round, and Olive. I don't like big dinners. Leave it to me, I'd fast forward to Easter. People pushing and shoving round Queen's Market in Santa hats, buying Brussels sprouts like there's no tomorrow. There was this woman down there yesterday, selling cigarette lighters that look like mobile phones, £1.99, and there was nearly blood shed because she was down to her last few. Grown women scrapping over fag lighters. And they've been playing 'Frosty the ruddy Snowman' down there since about October. I swear.

I thought I'd put a few things in a bag. Then, if he ever came to fetch this Goofer, I could sound him out. I'd be ready for a fast getaway, down to the seaside. Somewhere loonies don't smile at you through your kitchen window.

Christmas Eve morning he showed up. I said, 'I'd given you up for dead.'

'About right, too,' he said, 'I haven't been well, Bird. Flu jab turned nasty.'

I said, 'What are you doing for Christmas?'

'Thanks all the same,' he said, 'but I'm fixed up. People I know out at Chadwell Heath. They're expecting me and Freda this afternoon.'

I said, 'I was thinking I might come and give Brighton a try.'

'Yes,' he said, 'sounds all right to me. Course, I don't know when I'll be back down there. Could be a while yet. I'll give you a bell.'

I said, 'You got my number?'

'Yeah,' he said.

I don't think he has. He just put her lead, on, and the little overcoat I'd bought her. Never even said thank you. Never even brought me so much as a Toblerone.

He was out of the door, and then he came back. 'And by the way,' he said, 'anybody asks, you haven't seen me.'

The phone rang about two. I only answered it in case it was Clarice, might have had a bad turn or something, but it was Olive. 'Can you come, down?' she said. 'Only I've bought a mobile phone in Queen's Market for £1.99, and I can't get it to work.'

I don't know what made me go down to the garden that time in the afternoon. It was starting to get dark, and there was Wilf on his little folding chair.

'Looks like somebody's jumped on the roses,' he said. 'Here, take the weight off your feet.' Always a gentleman, Wilf.

He said, 'I was just thinking I'd come up and see you. I was just thinking I should put you in the picture.'

I said, 'Giving up on the garden?' I wouldn't have blamed him. My heart had gone out of it since they set light to my magnolia.

'No,' he said. 'About me and Blanche. Has she said anything?'

I knew he went round there sometimes.

'I've asked her to marry me,' he said, 'and she's said she'll have me.'

I knew Clark had got very fond of him.

He said, 'I've phoned our Susan, this morning. So now we're telling people.'

I knew Blanche had been buttering him up, sitting down in that shed, pretending to read his seed catalogues.

'Only I thought I should be the one to tell you,' he said, 'seeing as how . . . I mean, it could have been us, if things had worked out. I mean, we did talk about it, once upon a time.'

It's true. I only had to say the word.

I said, 'I hadn't realized.'

'No, well,' he said, 'you've had other things on your mind, with Jimmy turning up like that.'

So that's it.

He said, 'I knew there was no sense me hanging on, not once he was back on the scene.'

I said, 'Jimmy's not back on any scene.'

'That's as maybe,' he said, 'but I'm not going to come between husband and wife. Anyway, that's neither here nor there. Blanche is a lovely woman. She's good and kind and I couldn't do better.'

She's too young for him. They're all the same, men. Always trading in for the new reg.

I said, 'What does Clark say about it?'

'Oh, he's grand,' he said. 'And it'll keep me young, having a lad like that about.'

147

It will. Till his voice breaks and he starts wearing those saggy trousers, staying out half the night.

He said, 'You're not saying much. You're not upset, are you?'

Why would I be?

I said, 'Course I'm not upset. I wish you all the best, Wilf. I really do.'

'That's what I want to hear,' he said.

I said, 'When's it to be?'

'Easter,' he said. 'Blanche has got her heart set on Easter.'

His time of life I'd have thought they'd just get on with it. The way he's out on that allotment in all weathers, touch of bronchitis and she could have missed the boat.

I said, 'You'll move in before then, though? Save on your winter heating?'

'Oh no,' he said. 'Heating's only money. You've got to do things the right way. We've got to think about Clark. Everybody living over the brush now-adays; I don't hold with it. These youngsters don't see enough of people doing the right thing.'

He said he thought the roses might be all right – only time would tell. He said they'd be going up West the day after Boxing Day, to buy Blanche an engage-ment ring. He said I was invited for sherry and a mince pie Christmas morning, and they wouldn't take no for an answer, I never did like sherry. I don't see why they couldn't just leave everything the way it was. Why they couldn't just stay friends and Wilf keep his place. They might be glad of it. Sitting in a shed with somebody for an hour every now and then isn't like living with them, and Wilf does snore. I heard him once, in his fireside chair, having five minutes after dinner. Right through the window I could hear him. She'll find out. And Olive's going to miss her, because bingo every night'll be a thing of the past.

'No hard feelings then?' he said.

I told him not to be so daft. What would I want with another husband? I've got my memories.

We were all right as we were, though. Now Wilf's marrying Blanche, and Clarice's being sent to the holding pen, and it's like a graveyard next door, with Snake Eye gone and his bongo music. And Dwyer's gone off with the Goofer. All that's left of her is her squeaky Bill Clinton she liked to chew on and the extra Guinness I'd fetched in for her. I don't know, all kinds of things are starting to stop.

From my landing I counted thirteen electric winking Rudolfs. I wish I had an air gun.

Clark said, 'I'm getting a grandad, Mrs Gibbs.'

'So I heard,' I said, 'and what do you think about that?'

'Brilliant,' he said. 'Now I'll have someone to show my card tricks while Nan's at bingo.'

Card trick. He only knows one. He keeps saying he's got a new one to show me. Then he says, 'I think I'd better practise it a bit more, in case it goes wrong.'

That Jen wanted to know when was my birthday. I told her, I don't bother with anything like that any more. I'm either seventy-four or seventy-five, but I haven't been keeping proper count. I'm all right. Still feel about sixteen really, apart from getting out of puff and my legs hurting first thing and my ears not being A1. My skin's got too big as well. Apart from that, I'm grand.

'Oh,' she said, 'you mustn't be like that about birthdays. I've got a feeling you're a Capricorn.' Then she turned up on Tuesday with a sponge cake. 'I'm honouring your progress through life,' she said. And she'd brought a bottle of that water she's always drinking. Paying for water in a bottle. I never touched the stuff, even when it was free.

So she lit the candle and it played 'Happy Birthday'. Now that is progress. I'd love to know how they do that.

'Make a wish,' she said. I wished for a palm tree outside my window and a new pair of ankles.

'No,' she said, 'you're not meant to tell anybody what you're wishing. It's unlucky. Do it again, only this time, don't say it out loud.'

She's round the bend. You don't get what you wish for in this life. You get what you get. I coaxed her off the water with that bottle of coffee-crème drink Blanche and Wilf gave me at Christmas. Then she started. Half a toilet roll she'd gone through before I could get any sense out of her.

The thing was, it was *her* birthday. And this Flick she lives with wouldn't cancel her badminton.

'Rituals are so important in our lives, Birdie,' she said. 'And I cooked Flick her favourite dinner when it was her birthday.'

I said, 'Well, maybe she's got something in mind for tomorrow night.'

Another black eye, that's what I thought. Grown woman like that, carrying on about birthdays. She had two pieces of my cake.

'My friend Dee,' she said. I'd heard about her before. She's the one that goes on marches and won't have anything to do with men. She's the one borrowed a van to go to Avebury, wanted to hug some hill or something, and the fan belt came off and she couldn't even fix it herself; spent an hour in a phone box trying to find a woman mechanic.

'My friend Dee thinks I'm avoiding happiness,' she said. 'What do you think?'

I said, 'I think you do too much wondering. Too much sitting around thinking about yourself.'

She says she works, but it's not what I'd call a job. All she does is a bit of mumbo-jumbo with branches, burning oil in people's houses, chanting all over the place and worrying about what she eats. They have too many things to choose from these days: too many kinds of Cook-in Sauce, too many washing powders. I went into that big place in Stratford once, and I came over dizzy just looking at them. And all these fancy new ways of dying. Every week Olive's got a new one for me from her magazine. Ask me, we were better off when it was just meat and potatoes every night. Then it was either the big C or your heart stopped. That's all folks!

She said, 'Dee thinks I should try rebirthing. I might do. Dulwich isn't easy to get to without a car, though.'

She said it was nice to sit in my flat for five minutes, because their place is full of bad energy.

I said, 'Why don't you get the electric people out to have a look at it?' But apparently that wasn't what she meant.

She said, 'You see, Birdie, everything in the whole world, everything in the whole universe, is just electrons. Endlessly vibrating particles. That's all everything is.'

I knew what she meant. I felt like that myself after three of those coffee-crèmes.

It's two bus rides and then a walk up a great long hill to visit Clarice. I managed three times last week, but it's doing me in. Blanche and Wilf said they'd go once a week, but there's nobody else I can ask. Olive's struggling around on sticks, and the nice Indian lady along her landing has got kiddies to fetch from school. You can't go visiting at Lime Trees if you've got anything else to do with your life.

Sometimes when I go, she's got her shopping list ready, as if she's still in Cherry Tree. Next time, she might not even talk to me. They have their own rooms, and she's got her photos on her night table, but they don't like them shutting themselves away during the day. There's nowhere to sit anyway, only on your bed. Daytime they have to be in the day lounge, chairs all in a big circle, like wagon trains – Cherokee are after me – and that ruddy telly's never turned off. Nobody's watching it, only a few visitors, when they've run out of things to say. It's on from *Kilroy* in the morning till they get their Ovaltine just before the nine o'clock news, and if you try even just turning the sound off you get a right tongue-lashing from the supervisor. It's no wonder Clarice has gone all glassy-eyed. She used to do crosswords and all sorts. She used to listen to her tapes and sing along to all the psalms.

I think they have bingo some nights. Don't know what they'd win, though. An extra custard cream? A top-up of Ovaltine? No point in playing if there's nothing to win. No point in playing even if there is. And they have a woman comes in most Wednesdays, does shampoo and sets and keeps them looking nice. Clarice always had pretty hair.

So sometimes she nods off while I'm there and I wonder why I've bothered, and sometimes she wants to know all about the Fruit Bowl and how Clark's getting on and Olive and everyone. But most days now she just sits there. I could tell her anything. I do. I told her I sat next to Burt Lancaster on the 158 and she never batted an eyelid.

She's quietened down a lot from when they first took her there. First week she was there she played hell about having to sit with men. Not surprising, either. Clarice has led a very sheltered life, and there's no telling what you'll see in that day lounge.

All I hope is, when she's just sitting there and I'm

talking to myself, she's got something nice going through her mind. I hope she's thinking about that wine she had in Naples and wearing tinsel in her hair.

I went up there today. Took her some barley sugars and some magazines, and a tin of talc from Nellie at the chemist's. No sense in taking flowers, how hot they've got it in there, and you can't open the windows. Maximum security. They don't want anybody slipping out and calling it a day. They don't want anybody doing their own thing. It's like a boiler room in there. It's no wonder they all keep dozing off. Tax-payers' money and those carers are walking round in short sleeves. Middle of February and all that supervisor's got on under her uniform is a pair of knickers, plain as the nose on my face.

A girl came round with a clipboard while I was sitting there. 'Now, Clareece,' she said, 'have we had our bowels open today?' Eighteen or nineteen, she'd be. They all get to be such a size nowadays. I suppose it's since they brought in vitamins.

Clarice was trying to remember about her bowels. I said, 'Just say yes,' but she wouldn't.

The girl said, 'Because we didn't go yesterday, did we?' In front of all those people.

If they ever put me away, I shall be the baddest bugger they ever came across. I'd mess my knickers every time if I was spoken to like that.

I was just putting my coat on. She said, 'I'll be glad when it's time to go home, Birdie. Is it time yet?'

I said, 'You stay put. It's cold enough to freeze hell outside.'

She said, 'Are my plants all right? Are you watering them?'

It wasn't really a lie to say yes. Wilf and Blanche had most of them. Olive had a begonia, and Herbie took the Swiss cheese plant for his wife.

She said, 'I think I'll be home tomorrow. Do you know where they put my coat?'

Poor Clarice. They soon cleared her place out. They sent two men in – went through the whole flat in one day, painted over that Community Awareness mess, and there was one of those unmarried mothers in there by the Saturday, with a big fancy pushchair and a stud in her nose.

I said, 'You're better off in here – three meals a day and a nice warm room.'

White lies, that's all they are. Anybody pulls a stunt like that on me, though, I shall haunt them till kingdom come. The secret is to see it coming – when they start asking you if you know what year it is, you've got to jump before you're pushed. Early doors, before they wheel you into Lime Trees and start broadcasting your bowel movements on Capital FM.

'Birdie,' she said, 'do I have any shoes?'

The only place I could think of looking for him was the dog track. That Jen had tried to look him up in the Brighton phone book for me when she was at the library one time, but she couldn't find him. He probably hasn't even got a place in Saltdean. But there'd be people at Walthamstow who know him from way back when. Stewards and old kennel lads. They could tell me if they'd seen him around.

It's not him I'm bothered about. If I never clap eyes on him again, it'll suit me, but I often think about Vanessa and the Goofer, and I bet they've wondered about me as well. Wondered what happened to the lady with the choccie and the Guinness and the nice warm gas fire. They were good little pals to me, and I'd like to know how they're getting on, but the track's no fun on your own, and then there's that long walk in the dark from the bus.

But there's afternoon racing sometimes, so I thought of Clark, always mooching about when it's school holidays, always pestering for things to do.

I said, 'You know when it's half-term, how about coming with me to the dog track? See if we can find out what happened to those doggies?'

'Well,' he said, 'I don't know.'

I thought he'd jump at it.

I said, 'I'll pay.'

He said, 'I might be busy.' His voice is starting to break. He's still a nice boy, but he's changing.

I asked Blanche. I stay out of her way as best I can these days, because all I hear from her is how many calories in a lemon curd tart. She's trying to get a stone off before this wedding, so she's packed in the bingo and she's down at the slimming club three times a week. If I see her on the stairs, I see her, if I don't, I don't.

I said, 'What's his story? I thought he'd like a nice afternoon out. And he hardly ever comes round to see me any more.'

'Girls,' she said. 'He's just noticed them.'

Apparently there's one called Lorraine he's been seeing at Sunday school for a long time, because her dad's a lay preacher, and now they're getting to be so grown up they've both been bumped up to Bible-study leaders. And there's another one called Julie, from Clover Farm Estate, only twelve, but very advanced for her age.

Next time I saw him I said, 'You can bring your girlfriend too, if that's what's stopping you. My treat.'

He turned pink. He said he didn't think Lorraine'd be allowed. He said she has to help out at home when they're off school, and do extra practice on her clarinet, and anyway, her dad didn't hold with gambling. Her mum wasn't even allowed a lottery ticket.

I can understand that: the odds are ridiculous. If you're going to have a flutter, you want a sensible price at least.

I said, 'And what about this Julie? I bet she'd be allowed. Why don't you bring her round one day? I hardly see you nowadays.'

'Yeah,' he said.

I said, 'Clarice has gone and Olive's getting over her hip job, and now you've forgotten where I live. Am I using the wrong soap? Is there something I should know?' I don't know why I said all that. I didn't mean to. Being on my own doesn't bother me. And we all finish up that way, is how I look at it. Even Blanche. She might have Wilf Orme billing and cooing over her now, and Clark to cook for, but she'll come to it. We all do. Comes the day, you tidy away your newspaper after you've looked through it, and it stays tidied.

He turned pink again. He said he'd come with me to Stow, as long as we weren't too late back. He said he had things to do. Signed up for some thing at Aldersbrook — learning how to be a disc jockey. Can't see there's anything to learn, myself. You just tell them what you're going to play and then you play it. Ruddy funding for that, and they wouldn't even give us a garden seat. Anyway, he's the big man all of a sudden. People to see, places to go. Six months ago he was in my kitchen every afternoon, making paper aeroplanes and counting my biscuits. Now he's spraying his armpits every half-hour, according to Wilf. Squeezing his spots and getting shirty if Blanche goes in his room.

It's getting so bad along here, you think twice before you go out. The laundrette's been wrecked again, and there's been robberies. Broad daylight and they don't care. They put those cameras all over the estate, but it doesn't stop them. They think they're big telly stars, that's all, sunglasses on in the middle of the night, and the police do nothing but drive through. Ram-raiding, that's the latest thing. Smash the car into the front of a shop and then run off with the stuff. Some of those retards did it at Smart Mart, took somebody's car, drove it right in and took what they could carry. The value of that must have been in the tens of pounds. Let's face it, Smart Mart's no Mappin &

Webb. You'd think, if they were going to rob a place, they'd do it properly. Do one of these wireless shops. Park round the back with a getaway driver, inside man to let them in, and away with a van full of stereos, thank you and good night. That's how I'd do it. But they haven't got the brains they were born with.

That Tamsin's brother from Orange Grove is doing time for ram-raiding, and he never looked like he had two halfpennies to rub together, I walked past there, just after they'd put him away, and she was bragging to those Bloods, or Grievers they might have been, about him being banged up.

I said to her, 'Was it worth it, then? Has he bought himself a villa in Spain?' They looked at me.

I said, 'All this bobbing and weaving, and yet you never seem to have any money. There's not a one of you ever buys a nice suit and gets out of here. Nice pair of polished shoes and a fresh start in life.'

The little nervy one always does the talking. Can't stand still. He never stops twitching about. It might be a dance they do, or those lid poppers they take.

'We don't want no shoes shit,' he said.

I said, 'So what have you got? You going to be standing on street corners with a hanky on your head when you're forty?'

He said, 'We got levver. We got gold teef and stuff. Wanna stay out we personal business, lady, innit.'

To think, all those names on the memorials – the Brocks boys and Blue Catlin and Pearl and Olive's husband – all did their bit and never came home. Clarice's brothers, too, and what for? Save this crowd learning German? Bunch of wasters that wouldn't help you across Barking Road in a fog, never mind enlisting. Hitler wouldn't need his storm troopers if he came back today. A free CD and they're anybody's.

I could feel sorry for them, because they've got a whole lot of life left to get through, and they won't want to be down that arcade playing table football for ever more. Pity help them when they get to my age, that's all I say. Pity help them if they get to thirty.

Clark said, 'Mrs Gibbs, I've been thinking, I will come with you to look for the Goofer.'

'Good lad,' I said, 'and who's it to be, Lorraine or Julie?'

'No,' he said, 'they're not my girlfriends any more. I'm bringing Charlie.'

ATTENTION ALL BUDDING DJS!

Great news on the local teen scene. Aldersbrook Comprehensive's after-school DJ Workshops have proved so popular they'll be running again next term.

Workshop leader, Groovemeister Buzz, is a regular at the Bliss Bliss Club in Dagenham, and helped set up the DJ module of the National Performing Arts Diploma, which is now recognised as an NVQ.

He and Aldersbrook's head of Media Studies, Tatt Scanlon, will be on hand with advice on mixing, scratching and echoing.

Says Tatt, 'We aim to give kids insight into the basics of DJing, and to cover aspects like health and safety. And we always finish with a Club Nite, so they can take charge of the decks.'

Karl Tipper, 14, of Orange Grove tower says, 'It was wicked. I've been DJing just in my bedroom, but I might run my own club now.'

They were late. I said, 'Punctuality is the politeness of princes,' and he said he was sorry, but to tell the truth, he's not the boy he was. Ever since he got his new haircut, like a dead chrysanthemum dropped from a great height, that boy's been on the downward slide.

I didn't care much for her, either. A bit too knowing for my liking, and she never stopped chewing gum. I never heard so much noise from one stick of Hubba-Bubba. You could get up and dance to it. They named her Charlene after somebody on the telly, but everybody calls her Charlie. She lives in a maisonette on Clover Farm, and she gets ten pounds a week to spend on whatever she likes, so I suppose it's not just her body Clark's interested in.

I said, 'You realize you can't put your own bets on? If you want to have a little go, I'll have to go to the window for you to put your money on.'

'Well,' she said, 'my dad says I could easily pass for sixteen.'

That's the thing about them these days. They're wearing brassieres and got their own bleepers when we were still playing whip and top. Then, when they're really sixteen and they could go out and get a job, all they want to do is hang about the landings with £20 yo-yos.

'My dad', she said, 'sends me for his cigs, and I never have any trouble.'

I'd been waiting in for the council, but I told them I'd got to go out by eleven. Weeks I've been waiting for them to look at a great big crack in my bedroom wall. Dawn's got one as well, only she's not bothered. Since Snake Eye, she's not interested in anything. It's a terrible thing to see. As neighbours go she's been mainly trouble, but I don't like to see anybody go to pieces like that. And every time I see her shuffling down the health centre for her tranks it starts me off, trying to work something out – about that little baby me and Augie buried.

It was either 1954 or 55. I know it was after the Coronation, because I remember the bunting getting soaked and everybody packing into his Aunty Cis's back room, because she'd got a telly with a picture about the size of a postcard. I remember that day clear as if it was yesterday, and there definitely wasn't any baby on the scene then.

As I reckon it, she'd have been about forty now. And Dawn's only forty-five, and she looks like an old woman to me, now she's let the grey grow in. And then my brother Ted would be sixty-eight, and our dad would be a hundred and one, and there are plenty get to that age these days. There's two ladies in Lime Trees had hundredth birthdays since Clarice has been there. They had the mayor kissing them for a photo and a great big cake nobody could eat, because the icing was like carborundum and the raisin seeds get under their teeth.

So what it all amounts to is, there was me, and I was in my prime – nice loose Toni permanent and legs that used to drive men wild – there was that little baby, and there was my old dad. And yet, if they were here now, we'd all just be different kinds of old.

That's the kind of ruminating you do when you're waiting for the council to come and check you for subsidence.

I phoned the housing department again. Stupid jingle-jangle music they play, trying to drive you nuts, so you'll hang up and stop bothering them; keeping you holding on, pretending their girls are all busy. Busy deciding what to get off the tea trolley. Busy in the toilets doing their mascara. Clark said, 'It maybe

just needs a bit of filler. We could ask Uncle Wilf to
have a look at it.'

Wilf Orme's not setting foot inside my bedroom.
He had his chance.

We got there ten minutes before the first race and all
they could think about was chips.

There was one on the card called Lemon Squeezie.
Clark said, 'I'm picking her.'

'Him,' I said. 'Now sit still and listen to me; see
if you can learn something.' And then I told them
a few things: how some dogs'll always go for the
rail and some will always run wide, how some of
them come shooting out of their trap like wet soap,
and some of them wander out like they just woke
up.

Clark said, 'Can I get another Pepsi? I'm going to
bet on the ones with good names. No, I'm going to
bet on the fastest ones.'

Charlie said, 'I'm not. You've got to think about
the bends.' She was streets ahead of him already. I
might have taken to her, if it hadn't been for the gum.

I got them their drinks and put their bets on, and
then I went down among the bookies to see what I
could find out. Actually, I thought I might see him
down there. He could have been pencilling for somebody, or just hanging about. You get a lot of old boys

down there, looking at the runners, listening out for a whisper. Once you've worked with those dogs, you can't seem to stay away from them.

I asked Fly Lennie. Him and Dwyer go back to before the Ark. I don't know if he hadn't seen him, or if he just couldn't hear what I was saying. Anyway, he shook his head, and I didn't bother quizzing him any more. He's always got stuff in his eyes, like he's got a bad cold. You don't want to look at it, but you just can't stop yourself.

I asked Conroy's legman, but he was in a hurry, and then I spotted Blackie Smith. He was only a kid, hanging about, begging for jobs, when Jimmy first got his trainer's licence, and he's not a lot bigger now, except for round his middle. I don't know that he remembered me.

'No idea,' he said, then he had a bit of a think. He said, 'He might be doing something at the flaps. Have you asked round any of them? You could ask at Ganniford Down, make a few enquiries. I think I might have heard something about him.'

I hadn't even thought of that. Man of Jimmy's standing at one of those joints. More monkey business going on there than at a chimps' tea party.

I said, 'Who from?'

He said he couldn't remember, picking between his teeth with his train ticket.

He said, 'It was just a story going round before Christmas. It could have been some other Jimmy.'

I said, 'What was the story?'

He said, 'I think it was a ringer.'

'At Ganniford Down?' I said. 'A changeling dog?'

'Might have been,' he said. 'Or Gravel Lane. I don't know. Nothing to do with me.'

I said, 'Has he been here lately?'

'Don't know,' he said. 'I've been away. Had walking pneumonia. Are you his girlfriend?'

I said I was. I wrote my number down for him. Asked him to let me know if he heard anything. Waste of pencil lead.

He said, 'Why? Has he got you in the family way?' Laughing like a jackass, he was.

I'd told them to stay where I left them, but they'd moved, and they weren't even facing the track when I found them. They'd fetched more chips and there they were, sitting with their backs to the dogs, because they hadn't won anything. Couldn't be bothered. And that's how they stayed till I got a tickle in the sixth race. Then they were my new best friends. Then they wanted me to mark their card.

There was an old geezer taking an interest as well, sitting just along from us. More hair growing out of his ears than on his head.

'Having a day out with the grandkiddies?' he said.

I hadn't done anything to encourage him. I could see he was on sticks, and I'm looking for a man that can do the Continental.

He wanted to give me a tip for race eight. 'Judge Bean,' he said. 'Can't fail.' I wouldn't mind a fiver for every time I've been told that. I wouldn't turn my nose up at a pound for every time. Hear them talk about some of these dogs, you'd think they could walk on water. Then they run, and you find out. He was off colour. He got bumped. He had the legs of it, but he's no good when there's an R in the month.

Jimmy did have a dog at Brighton, an open racer, Neversay. He was the nearest I ever saw to perfect — big ugly brindle, but he ran every race like he meant it. Then he had a broken hock that wouldn't mend, so they put him to stud and nothing happened. They didn't get a single pup out of him. That's the thing with dogs; there's always something.

Charlie said, 'How much longer does this go on for?'

Clark said, 'We can't go yet. We've got to find the Goofer.'

I told him I'd drawn a blank. I wasn't going to get into all that business about Jimmy. If he's really doing the flapping tracks, it couldn't be anything kosher. There's a scam a minute at Gravel Lane, and Ganniford

Down's no better. He'll be up to naughties, or I'm the Queen of Sheba.

I didn't back Judge Bean just to spite that old geezer, so of course it walked it.

'Told you it couldn't fail,' he said.

I told him to go sit on his stick.

That Charlie said, 'Where's the gift shop? Are we going to get a T-shirt or something? How much do these dogs cost?'

I told her.

'Yeah,' she said, 'my dad'd buy me one, no problem.'

Clark was catching flies with his mouth.

She said, 'Right, I've got an idea. What happens to them afterwards? What happens to these dogs after they're all worn out?'

But I wasn't going to talk about that.

I fancied a bit of sea air, that's all. I could have gone to Southend, but Brighton made more sense. Take a walk down memory lane, have a look at what they've done to the pier. It wasn't anything to do with Jimmy Dwyer. And I needed a day off from Blanche and Olive. Weddings, weddings, weddings, is all I've heard since Christmas Day. All that fuss at their time of life. I'm surprised at Wilf Orme, and that's a fact.

I was up at six, had two Nescaffs and then went down as soon as Kareem had opened up, to get a paper and my Twixes. That Jen was down there, buying juice, and she's no morning glory.

She said, 'It's my biorhythms, Birdie. Since Flick went I can't sleep.'

To this day I don't know what made me get off that tube at Tower Hill. I could have gone straight through to Victoria, onto one of those fast trains, and been first through the doors of the Richmond for elevenses.

I'd only been thinking a bit, rattling in from Upton Park, how it's all like a train ride, really, life and everything. You get on, and you know you'll be getting off some time, but you can't be certain when it'll be. There could be signals failure; you could be stuck at Mile End with the doors open and not be able to understand a word they're saying on the bing-bong, or at Whitechapel. They've all got men talking through tea towels; people with saucepans over their heads making the announcements.

You get in, and there's people sitting there already. You can't choose who it'll be. Your mum and dad, aunties, brothers. All that. Just like on the trains, you never know who you'll get. Kiddies and old-timers, nutters drinking Special Brew at half past eight in the morning. I saw that Derek Jameson once.

And then, every time the train stops, some get out and you never see them again, and some new ones get in. You might not like the look of some of them, but sometimes people turn out nicer than you thought. By the time you get to where you're going, there probably won't be anybody left that you started with. And that's life. By the time you get to East Putney, though, you know you're nearly at the end of the line.

I think that was what made me think about that little baby. First stop and she was off. Hardly worth getting on really.

I got the Circle Line round to St Pancras. Now that's another way of looking at life. That Jen swears she's been round two or three times already. She's been an ancient Roman and an Egyptian princess, and now she's in Almond Blossom with rising damp.

I'd just made my mind up, all in a flash, and then after I'd bought the ticket I couldn't think what possessed me, going all the way up there, when I could have had a nice walk along Marine Parade. Going looking at gravestones, when I could maybe have found a little tea dance somewhere.

I wouldn't have known Leicester. The market's all done up like a dog's breakfast and Woolies has gone from Gallowtree Gate. It's all precincts now. Everywhere's precincts and opticians and fifty different kinds of coffee. And the Belgrave Road – I thought I'd made a wrong turn, fairy lights strung all over it, and curry places. I think it was the smell that made me come over faint. I just needed to lean for a minute. I was all right, but a little brown boy came over, with his hair in a bun and a doily on it. I think he was a boy, but these days you never know.

He said, 'You all right, lady?' Talking English just like you and me.

I got a taxi to Gilroes, just to the main gate. I thought I'd be able to get my bearings from there. Right, then straight on, then left and over a bit. There's a lot of people been buried since 1954.

I couldn't find it, so I had to go back to the office. He was a nice man in there, but I started him off on the wrong tack. I told him Gibbs. I just didn't think. And then, when he couldn't find it, I suddenly thought.

I said, 'No. It'll be under Borders.'

He said, 'Now are you sure?' All exasperated.

Of course I was sure. They see a few wrinkles and they treat you like you're retarded.

I said, 'It might have been 1955. And there might be somebody in there with her by now.'

'Oh yes?' he said. 'And what name would that be?'

'Mr Borders,' I said. 'We lost touch.'

She was further over to the left than I'd remembered, and five rows in from the footpath. I'd never have found it just wandering round. First time I'd been there in forty years. I'd bought some daffs from the stall down at the front gate, but she'd already got a nice pot plant, so somebody had been looking after her. And Augie's name wasn't on the stone. Be funny, I thought, if he turned up the very same day; if he happened to come along, and there's me, standing there like a spook.

I didn't know what to say to her. I mean, I hardly knew her, and I think I know how things would have panned out. I don't think I'd have been cut out for it: playing dollies' hospitals and sticking her crayonings up on the wall, like Blanche used to with Clark. Forking out for shoes every five minutes, and having to cook a proper tea every night. Mash it all up, spoon it in. Here comes the aeroplane, one for the Queen. Augie would have liked all that. And then she'd have started going out dancing. I'd have been stuck at home, and he'd have been pacing the floor in case there was some boy up to no good with her. There'd have been words. And then she'd have moved in with somebody and broken her father's heart, and had little babies and come round expecting me to mind them. Turning up with high chairs and jack-in-the-boxes, and promising she'd only be an hour. I can see it all.

Course, she might have been very bright. Her dad was. He had lovely handwriting, and he knew all his dates: Battle of Naseby, Great Fire of London, Christopher Columbus. She might have done well in life, been a manager and got one of those executive homes, or got her own pub. Then again, she might have made the grade, say she'd been born a few years later. When you see what they can do nowadays. Growing babies in test-tubes. Freezing people like sides of beef, for when they invent some miracle cures.

By rights, I could go in that plot when the time comes. It was Augie's Aunty Cis made us get it. Great long bus ride to get to it, if you were inclined to go visiting graves, which all that family were. But she said it was in a very good position. She said a nice family plot was always a good investment. They were funny like that, the Borders. Always buying savings certificates, and insurance policies. And yet, when I went out and bought a little cerise coat out of my own hard-earned money, I never heard the end of it. Only a nice little swing-back duster coat, it was, and you'd have thought I'd flushed fifteen guineas down the toilet.

I was just thinking about getting back to the station when a woman arrived, three graves up; she'd brought her own pan scourer to get the moss off and a plastic bag for the dead leaves.

I said, 'Are you here often?'

She looked at me.

I said, 'I don't suppose you ever see anybody at this grave, do you? See who brought the plant?'

'Don't think so,' she said.

I said to her, 'Tall, slim gentleman, with a very upright bearing?'

'Mm,' she said.

'Probably brings a prayer book with him,' I said. 'Blue eyes, quietly spoken.'

'Mm,' she said.

I said, 'So you have seen him?'

'No,' she said, 'I already told you I haven't.'

Time-wasting muttonhead. Creeping round cemeteries with a dustpan and brush, getting people's hopes up.

It was nearly seven o'clock by the time I got home,

and my belly thought my throat was cut. Blanche was yoo-hooing me on the stairs. 'Where've you been?' she said.

'Nowhere,' I said. Never did get my plate of cockles and half an hour in a deckchair. Spent all that money and ended up about as far from the sea as a body can go, and I was still none the wiser about Augie or Jimmy Dwyer or anything else. Talking to a hole in the ground. I must want my bumps feeling. At least with Clarice she does sometimes answer you back.

Blanche said, 'Are you all right, Birdie? You look all in.'

Nothing half an hour in front of my gas fire couldn't fix. My Tog-Tastic eiderdown and a bar of Fruit & Nut. Stop dwelling on graveyards and little babies that probably never even opened their eyes.

Margaret Anne, we named her, or Augie did, after his mother.

If it had been left to me, I wouldn't have gone. I've been to enough weddings. But Blanche wanted me there and Wilf wanted whatever Blanche wanted, so that was that. So it was going to be Herbie Ford and Olive for witnesses, me and Clark, and Wilf's girl, Susan, if she could get the time off work. Olive wanted us to put a spread on for them at her place – sausage rolls, pineapple chunks on sticks, that kind of thing.

She said, 'We could manage it, Birdie. You could do the sandwiches.' But I had a quiet word with Blanche and she agreed with me. Easiest thing was to nip across to the Samuel Pepys, a round of drinks, a round of ploughman's, and then her and Wilf could cab it to Paddington and the rest of us could get the train home. Course, Olive can never leave well alone. She had to turn up with a big tin of fairy cakes, in case the pub had run out of stuff to eat. In case there was a worldwide shortage of cheese-and-onion crisps.

Thursday night, Susan phoned Wilf to say they'd got five off with diarrhoea and sickness so she wouldn't be able to come. Blanche read more into it than there was; thought it was about wicked step-mothers and all that. She thought they all should have piled down, the husband and the grandchildren. I said, 'Blanche, he never sees them from one year to the next. Wasting money on petrol, all the way down those motorways to spend ten minutes in Hackney Town Hall. It's hardly the wedding of the year.'

She said, 'It's the wedding of *my* year.'

I said, 'Well, that's as it should be. You and Wilf can just do your own thing. No need getting involved with a bunch of relations. Getting frosty looks because you might not be as perfect as the first Mrs Sainted Evelyn Orme.'

'Yes,' she said, 'you're right. And I have seen photos, so I do feel like I've met them.'

I've seen photos too. I think Blanche forgets sometimes, about me knowing Wilf, long before she was on the scene. Big scruffy bunch, they are. You can't tell the girls from the boys. All in black anoraks and muggers' hats, even in their Christmas photo for their grandad. Nobody knows how to dress any more. You never see a nice little brooch on anybody's lapel.

They'd booked up ten days in Torquay, bed, break-fast and evening meal, so Blanche had asked me to keep an eye on Clark.

He said, 'There's no need for me to be minded, you know, Nan. I'm old enough to stop on my own.'

I said, 'You've changed your tune. It's only five minutes ago you were forever angling to spend the night on my couch.'

He doesn't like to be reminded of all that, not now he's the big man about town, with his combat trousers.

It was a beautiful morning. The rain stopped and the sun bounced up that bright off the wet road it hurt your eyes. Blanche put her own curlers in and then Nellie from the chemist's came over to comb her out.

She said, 'Did you hear that carry-on last night?'

There'd been a big party, somewhere along Blackberry Hedge, but of course our bedrooms face the other way. Nellie said the police had come because of the noise, but it was about ten to one, morons to coppers, so they'd just given them a warning and then driven off. Warnings.

I said, 'They're a laughing stock round here, the police. We might as well have a couple of cardboard cut-outs dotted around and save on the wages. Pictures of Jack Warner.'

Olive said, 'Well, they have to be careful these days. They can't just go round arresting people, not somewhere like this. That's why we've got community policing. Keep everything nice and calm.'

Community policing. I can tell you who's in charge on this estate and it isn't Mr Plod. Nellie said you could smell the Mary Jane from inside her lounge with the windows shut tight.

Blanche said, 'See? And that's why you have to be minded, Clark. Maybe you should come to Torquay with us. It'd be all right with Uncle Wilf.'

He said he wasn't going, didn't matter what anyone said.

I said, 'What about me, Blanche? If you don't mind extras tagging along? I think I'd be safer in Torquay.'

Olive said, 'Oh no, Birdie, that'd never do.'

You can never have a joke with Olive. You'll be there all day explaining it.

I said to Clark, 'And I suppose you think playing nursemaid to you is my idea of a treat? I suppose you think it's me that'll be stopping *you* having a good time? I suppose you're worried how you're going to get through ten days without greens for your dinner?'

He's hard work compared to what he used to be, but I did get a little smile out of him.

Blanche did look lovely, I must say, once she'd hauled herself into her roll-on. A nice navy suit from Evans and a straw hat. The skirt was longer than I'd have had it, but her ankles aren't anything to write home about, so it was probably for the best.

Olive said, 'Now what about something borrowed? Would you like my real pearl pendant?' Real out of a Christmas cracker. I showed her once how you're supposed to bite on them to see if they're the genuine article, and the pearl stuff started peeling off.

'And something old?' she said. 'I've got a little lacy hanky I've had for years.'

I said, 'She doesn't need any more antiques. She's got Wilf.'

Herbie Ford had got the rings. He was on bride-groom detail, once the nurse had been in to turn his wife. That's how every day is for him now, waiting for the nurse, laying out all the pills in little pots, having to get somebody in to sit with her if he's going any further than the Wavy Line. He could get her in somewhere, but he won't hear of it.

He said to me once, 'She never complains, Birdie. All she's been through, and she still manages a smile.'

All I hope is, if I'm going to end up like that, I get the early-warning signs. Go for a walk in a blizzard. I may be gone some time. Everybody says that, though, while they can still do cartwheels. 'If I ever get like that,' they say, 'put a pillow over my face.' Easier said than done, I suppose. That's why we all end up lying around, staining the mattress.

Anyway, Herbie phoned, just before zero hour. He said, 'I've got one bridegroom here, all present and correct, just wants to check which side his carnation ought to be pinned. And the post's just come, so please will you tell Blanche they've got a gift voucher from Susan and family.'

I said, 'Why doesn't he tell her himself? She's only sitting here having her eyebrows done.'

'No,' he said, 'it might bring bad luck. We'll see you there.'

Olive had got them towels, Clarice had sent them a postal order, and I'd given them a great big teapot, like a country cottage, with the chimney for a spout, because they both drink tea till it's coming out of their ears.

Me and Clark ran into Poundstretcher to find some confetti and, when we came out, there was Olive giving us the hurry-up.

'They've gone in without us,' she said. 'Messing around shopping. Now we'll have missed half of it.'

I told her. 'They've just gone in to settle up. They can't start without you. They've just gone in to swear there's no just cause and pay the bill.' There's not much I don't know about weddings.

You can have music now. Take your own tape in. They had Frankie singing 'I Didn't Know What Time it Was'. That took me back. Lovely easy voice he used to have. I got a bit choked up, to tell the truth, because the last time I heard him, he was having to sidle up to some of those notes and grab hold of them as best he could. Everything seizes up. You can't sing any more, can't do hooks and eyes, can't even get in and out of the bath without having the Marines on standby. The only thing you get better at is complaining.

But Wilf looked so smart, you could see your face in his shoes. That's the Army for you. Stand still long enough around Wilf and you'll end up either blancoed or polished to a shine. And he wouldn't leave go of Blanche, hanging on to her arm like she might disappear any minute. Love's young dream. And when they stood up to put the ring on and everything, Clark nudged me. 'Hands together and eyes closed, Mrs Gibbs,' he said. He kills me, that boy.

Sunday me and Clark went to the London Dungeon, every kind of torture ever invented, with sound effects and everything. Wilf's treat. Olive was looking out for us, yoo-hooing from her landing when she saw us coming across the Fruit Bowl.

'We're in the papers,' she said. 'In the coloured weekend magazine, with photos and everything.'

Her Brian's lady friend goes cleaning in Island Gardens, some big fancy flat the size of Wembley Stadium, and they give her their old newspapers, if she wants them. I used to get the magazines from her sometimes, for Clarice.

Olive said, 'It's called "Rotten Fruit" and it's all about how we're the worst estate in London.'

I said, 'Well, that's nice. Why don't they put a sign up as well, down at the bus stop – "Abandon Hope All Ye Who Enter Here". Worst estate in London.

How am I ever going to get anybody to swap flats with me?'

She said, 'No, but this is according to somebody that's studied up on it. It's all in here. All the facts and figures. They reckon it's a powder keg, waiting to go up. And I hope it does, then I can go to the nursing home, like Clarice.'

She thinks she'd see more of Brian if she was in Lime Trees. She thinks she'd be quids in without her bills to pay. She doesn't realize they take your pension book.

I had a look at the magazine. It was about the gangs, mainly. They should have asked me or Wilf. We could have told them about our little garden, and about picking up the litter and trying to make a decent life for yourself. But good news is no news. They never even told us they were coming. They told the Billies and the Bloods, though. Wrote them up – three pages of it. But you couldn't tell who'd said what because they'd all got daft names: Moosa, Sugar, DOA. The only one I knew for sure was that Tamsin, because of her scar. Juice, she calls herself now. It was all about hand signs and not letting anybody onto their patch, specially not the police, and how they're all big buddies looking out for one another, because society has failed them. That's what you get when you send an ologist round with a tape-recorder.

Monday we hardly moved all day, it was so warm. First Easter I can ever remember when it didn't blow a gale or snow.

Started off, I took a chair down to the garden, but somehow I can never settle there. You don't get the sun for long down there, because of the towers, and once it's in shadow, I don't care for it. It gives me the shivers. That Jen gave it a going-over, after the business with Snake Eye, clapping her hands and ringing her gongalong bells. She said it should be all right after that, and the crocuses are nice. They've come popping up, even if everything else has gone for firewood, but I still don't like it down there.

So I went back up on the landings, to try and catch a few rays, and Patti brought a chair out as well. Sat there just in her undies, so I sent Clark down to Kareem's to fetch ice cream. Boy his age sees a woman in her brassiere, there's no telling where it'll lead. I leaned over the railing and watched him till he was out of sight. He's got one of those black woolly hats as well, makes everybody look like a wanted poster. They're regulation issue round here.

I said, 'Aren't you boiled under that tea cosy?'

He swore he wasn't. His face looked like a little tomato, but he swore he needed his hat.

I was just saying to Patti that, considering some of the stories I'd been hearing, I hadn't seen a policeman in days, when the sirens started. Police first, then an ambulance, and after a bit there was a helicopter as well – wup-wup-wup – till you couldn't hear yourself think. Nearly an hour Clark was gone, and when he did come back he was empty-handed. I said, 'And where's my choc ice?'

'Sorry, Mrs Gibbs,' he said, 'but a little girl got cut, because the police were in the laundrette and the window got smashed, and they've taken Big Dwayne away in a van, and a lady away in a car, and now the Bloods say there's going to be real trouble, because it was unnecessary force. So your ice cream melted. My nan won't half be mad when she finds out she's missed all this.'

He hadn't actually seen any of it. It had happened while he was in the shop, and by the time he was out on the street everybody was telling a different story.

So then Patti roused herself to go down and get the facts. Put a scrap of a dress on, although, why she bothered I don't know, because there's not a man on this estate hasn't seen her in her knickers, and most of them have seen her out of them as well.

We'd gone indoors to watch *Neighbours* when she got back.

She said, 'It was a little girl called Jade that got cut. You'd know her. Her mum's Janice – skinny Janice, very nervy, lives in Orange Grove. They reckon there was blood everywhere. And Janice got arrested, same time as Big Dwayne, so Janice's sister had to go with Jade in the ambulance and nobody's heard anything. Nobody knows how she's doing; There's some Bloods and some Billies down in the garages, talking up a storm, and Kareem says they've had all the empty milk bottles from out the back of the Kabin, so he's shutting up early, going to visit family in Southall. Oh, and there's police all over Orange Grove. They're taking Janice's flat to pieces, by the looks of things.'

Clark wanted to fetch a video, but as soon as we set foot outside, we could hear there was something going on. There was quite a crowd outside Orange Grove and some of them had got sticks, banging on the police van. Patti was down in front of Apple Bough, with Dawn.

'Well,' she said, 'the latest is, Jade's had to have stitches – hundreds of them. Big Dwayne's not been seen, Janice is still at Barking Road nick and they've got stuff bagged up on her landing. It's all roped off. Dawn thinks it's bomb squad.'

Clark grabbed my arm. 'Monty,' he said. 'We shall have to go and fetch him.' Monty's Wilf's budgie.

I said, 'There's no bombs up there. They'd have had us all out of here by now if it was bombs. Cleared the area.'

Patti said, 'Oh, don't be so sure, Birdie. I've never seen so many police on the Fruit Bowl. All those men up there in boiler suits. It must be something serious.'

She's got such a mouth on her, that Patti. She could stir for England, I swear.

I promised Clark we'd check on Monty as soon as they started letting people through. I promised him faithfully we'd get *Honey I Shrunk The Kids* another time.

I said, 'We can still go to your nan's. We can watch *Spaceballs*. You like that.'

He pulled a face, but I had my way in the end. There's more to this childminding business than I'd realized.

Tuesday morning you could tell there was something up. People around I'd never seen before. Ten o'clock in the morning and the place was jumping. I went down to the Wavy Line and that Jen was just coming along, all excited.

'Have you heard?' she said. 'Those fascists won't let Janice visit her little girl. An innocent little girl like that in hospital, cut to ribbons, and those bastards won't let her mother out. We're marching on the police station. There's going to be trouble, mark my words.'

Listen to her, you'd think the circus was in town.

I said, 'Are you a friend of this Janice, then?'

'Nothing to do with it,' she said. 'You've just got to show solidarity.'

There were even some Billies up and about, and Bloods, round the back of the garages, busy with something. Not Bob-a-Job week, that's for sure.

I saw Nellie, queuing at the checkout. I said, 'What do you make of all this? They reckon there's going to be a protest march.'

'Agitators,' she said, 'That's what Mr W. reckons. Communist agitators. And it wasn't bombs she was making, it was crack cocaine. And that's definite. Mr W.'s got friends on the force, you know?'

Mr W. runs the chemist's.

We were on the main news at dinner time. Olive phoned and said, 'Switch it on, quick.'

They'd had nearly a hundred people outside the police station, doing Hitler salutes and waving placards. 'Suffer Little Children,' one of them said. I couldn't see that Jen anywhere, though. Couldn't see anybody I recognized, as a matter of fact. Then they had the police on. Some big noise with scrambled egg all over his uniform.

He said his officers had used reasonable force, the little girl was as well as could be expected, and a man and a woman were continuing to help the police with their inquiries. He said people should calm down and go home. He said they would continue to police the Fruit Bowl Estate with discretion and sensitivity.

The cavalry, that's what I wanted to see. Or the paras.

We could hear thunder rolling around, in the distance, and I was hoping for a good downpour, save me traipsing over to the allotments to water Wilf's spinach. Clear the pond life off the streets as well. It's a well-known fact that villains go home when it rains. But it never amounted to anything, just rumbling around, miles away, over Woolwich or Shooter's Hill.

Half past six, I said to Clark, 'We'll go now, straight there, straight back, and then stay in, in case they start anything.' But then Olive turned up.

She said, 'Apparently they found a great big crack in that Janice's flat. That's why they had it fenced off. And I've got one, too. A big new one in my bedroom ceiling. I've tried phoning the housing people, but it just rings out and rings out and nobody ever answers.'

I tried explaining to her, about the cocaine. 'Yes,

196

I know,' she said, 'and that poor little mite, all on her own in hospital because of it. And who was it that cut her, that's what I can't follow.'

Clark said, 'It was the window that cut her, when it broke, when they were trying to get Big Dwayne, when he was getting the drugs from Janice.'

'Yes, that's it,' she said. 'But what if it comes down on me in the night? The crack?'

I said, 'I suppose we'll find you flattened out under it, like a big slice of Spam, and you'll never have known what hit you.'

It was gone seven before we got rid of her.

There was a bit of noise coming from Aldersbrook side. It sounded like somebody banging on dustbins, only we have those big plastic wheelies now, so it couldn't have been. There were people out on their landings, cooling off, trying to see what was going on, and that Jen shouted down to us.

She said, 'They've got a police van rolled over, down near the health centre. Serve them right.'

I said to Clark, 'Pay no attention.'

You have to do the watering with a can. Wilf won't have a sprinkler, because you're supposed to pay for a permit or something. Who'd know? That's what I keep asking him. Lugging water up and down from that tank. He said, '*I'd* know, Birdie. It's against regulations.' Does everything by the book, Wilf. You can take the man out of the Army, but you can't take the Army out of the man. Blanche is welcome to him, as a matter of fact.

Clark did the lugging and I just told him where to sprinkle it. Time was he was a willing lad, but now he's forever looking at his watch. Always wanting to go out and see who's about, and he hasn't really got any friends, not round here. That Charlie, maybe, but I haven't heard her name for a while, and, of course, I'm not allowed to ask − strict instructions from Blanche − otherwise he goes off sulking in his room and he won't come out for hours. Happy days.

We were just finishing up when they started coming over the footbridge. Just a few for a start, and then a big mob of them, piling over from Clover Farm, all got their photofit hats on.

We set off home the long way round. I didn't want to get mixed up with any of those Grievers, looking for trouble. Probably been sniffing Harpic. Just as we turned the corner into Orchard Walk we could see smoke, and our local boys slowed down alongside us.

PC Smalley said, 'You want to get yourself home, Gran, and this young man. They've set fire to Mandela House, and there's cars alight across Bramble Dene. They've got it blocked.'

Then they got it through on their wireless, about Vine Road being closed as well. Two fire engines trying to get in and the no-necks had got barricades across. I didn't like the sound of that. Everybody likes a fireman. If they'll turn on them, they'll turn on anybody.

Then the drumming started. There was a crowd outside Orange Grove. Some of them had got staves, and some of them had got great shards of glass, and somebody had sprayed NARK and RIP across the front of that Janice's neighbour's flat. I couldn't see who was playing the tom-tom. Didn't want to. Drums of war, that's what it sounded like. Makes your blood run cold.

Clark said, 'I *told* you we should fetch Monty across to my nan's. He could get frightened all on his own, if he hears fire engines and things.' And before I could stop him he was heading over there, straight up to one of the hanky-heads.

I said, 'Clark, you do as you're told and come with me.'

I didn't want his nan coming back from her honeymoon and finding him in Whipp's Cross with a label tied round his toe.

He said to that boy Bone, 'What's happening? I've got to fetch my Uncle Wilf's budgie. Flat forty-seven.'

That Bone said, 'Eye for an eye, innit. People snake on people, they get they face glassed. They get they house torched.'

I didn't know what to do for the best. I was worried about being trapped up on the seventh if they were going round starting fires, but I didn't want us hanging about on the street.

The light was dropping fast. There was banging coming from Aldersbrook way, and whistles blowing and black smoke curling over, and drumming and yodelling outside Orange Grove. You'd never have thought you were in England. It was like something off the telly news. Occupied territories, that's us. Occupied by bottom-feeders. If only I'd had my handbag with me; if only I'd had a few bob in my pocket, we'd have been on a bus out of there, till it was all over. Up to Stratford for a nice film and a bag of Maltesers.

A big police van came squealing round from the main road, on two wheels near enough, and then another one right behind it. They stopped just past the Wavy Line and there must have been thirty of them got out – could have been more – truncheons, helmets, shields, the full regalia.

Jinks came running past with an armful of videos in those plain boxes, so then I knew they'd broken into MoviMajik. I said, 'I'll name you, you lowlife, when they come round asking. Robbing from a neighbour.'

He said, 'I never took them, I found them. I was given them. Bought them, for cash.' He was so loaded up he was nearly dropping stuff. The first time in his life he's ever moved faster than a slug, as well, work-shy waste of space.

Patti came down out of the lift and said it was on the wireless. Five police hurt, Mandela House gutted, and looting down at the chemist's.

I said, 'Well, let's send some vans out with loud hailers. Get down the tube stations and hand out flyers, make sure everybody knows about it. Then we'll have every pea brain in London here before the night's out. They'll be bussing them in. They'll be handing out wire baskets.'

Next thing, there were people coming all ways. Police running under the walkways, and firemen. More police running round by the road. Billies, Bloods, Grievers, mouth-breathers in camouflage jackets, faces I'd never seen before, and I know everybody. They were coming from behind Almond Blossom, and up between Orange Grove and Apple Bough. It was like somebody had kicked an ants' nest.

That decided me. I said, 'Home, Clark. We'll have to take our chance.' Then I noticed something.

Over at Cherry Tree, there were people moving about on the first landing, lots of them, too dark to make out because the lights over there haven't worked in weeks. I thought it was riot squad, the way they were creeping about. There wasn't a sound from them.

Then I saw a little flame up there, and something came flying through the air, whump! Down into the coppers. There was a smell of petrol, but no fire, and everything stayed quiet. Then it started. Brick ends raining down, and lumps of concrete, and bottles that had been set alight, and there was a boy screaming, with his trousers on fire, and men round him trying to put him out. Now there's a terrible sound. Worse than tom-toms, even.

Patti said, 'Let's get upstairs, quick! We'll be able to see better.' But when I turned round to get Clark, he wasn't there. I shouted his name, but he'd never have heard me over that racket, and I couldn't see him over all those heads. They say it's nice for a girl to be small and dainty, but not if you're going to see active service, it isn't. The things I could have done in life with another six inches.

Patti said, 'Perhaps he went up?' but I knew he hadn't.

I said, 'It's that bloody budgie, pardon my spelling. That's where he's gone. He's going to get himself killed, and the ruddy thing doesn't even talk.'

Wilf swears it says, 'Who goes there?' and 'Quick march,' but I've never heard it.

She said, 'Well, come up anyway. You'll be able to spot him from higher up.'

But I told her to go on up without me. I knew he

was down there somewhere, in that mayhem, and I couldn't go and leave him, after all I'd promised his nan.

They were carrying men away past us, down towards the rec, and there were still police coming in by Orchard Walk, but not as many of them as the scum that was rolling in from Blackberry Hedge. Types that look like they have to go for a lie-down after they've made a roll-up, full of beans all of a sudden, leaping around with spades and fence posts and mallets. A gap opened up for a minute, so I went for it. I thought perhaps if I could get round the back of Orange Grove I might be able to get up to Wilf's and find him. Hole up there for the night maybe – me, him and Monty the Mute. I wasn't feeling too special, to be honest. I think that's why I lost my bearings, with all the smoke and the shenanigans. I think I was going in circles in the end. Good job I did, else I wouldn't have run smack into that Jen.

'Birdie.' She was gasping. I thought she was going to have a heart attack on me. 'I saw Clark. I'm sure it was him. Went into the Kabin with some Bloods. They're in there ransacking, and the garages are on fire. It could go up any minute.'

I didn't know what to think. Clark's never had anything to do with the Bloods, and she could have seen anybody. I don't see how you could tell any of them apart on a clear day with a telescope, never mind in that smog. But Kareem had got Calor gas and all sorts behind that shop.

There were firemen there, trying to reel out a hose as near as they could get to the garages, but they hadn't got a hope in hell. It was raining boulders from the walkway, and there were kids with sticks and bats, two lines deep, between them and the ramp.

A boy came out of the Kabin, arms full of vodka bottles, and PC Smalley came running up, trying to collar him. He'd lost his helmet. Lost his wireless. Lost his oppo as well, because I couldn't see him anywhere.

He said, 'Get out of here. The fires are spreading. And don't use the lifts.'

That Jen said, 'Clark Fairbrother's in there with some Bloods, and Birdie's meant to be looking after him.'

I didn't even have time to open my mouth. She said, 'It *was* him I saw, Birdie. You tell me any other Blood that wears specs.'

Then there was a funny roar, like a train, and Kareem's front window blew out. Glass, then smoke, then flames.

It's the first five minutes that matter with a fire.

'Run for your lives,' he said. 'Run for your lives.' And he blew his whistle.

The blast broke their lines up enough for him to get past them, but by the time I could get my legs moving they'd packed close together again. Ruddy Armageddon let loose just behind them, and they were still more interested in beating up firemen. There were people screaming up on the walkways, thought they were going to be blown sky-high, and that Jen was fainting on me, hanging round my neck like a great walrus. I shoved her onto the ground. Nothing personal, she was halfway there anyway. Sometimes you just have to do things.

I couldn't get through them and I couldn't get round them. They were solid. So I elbowed two of them in the orchestra stalls. That did it, never fails. That moved them enough for me to squeeze through.

I thought I'd be able to crawl in there and try to find him. Keep low to the floor for air. Get him out before the fumes did him in. I did my best, but I'm not as young as I was. I did a whole lot better than some of them.

I pulled my cardigan up over my head, but that heat still smacked me across the face like an oven door. I counted. I thought if I could wriggle forward for ten and still be there, I'd try another ten. I'd got to twenty-seven when I found a pair of feet.

I lost it a bit after that. I was tugging on him, pulling him out after me, and I was getting there, but it was taking too long. He was a dead weight, and I was feeling with my feet for the doorway, just straight back the way I'd come, it should have been, but I couldn't find it anywhere. I thought we'd had it, actually, and I didn't really care. I know the ceiling came down, just ahead of me, but I couldn't tell you when that was exactly.

Next thing I knew, I was being poorly on the concrete in front of Almond Blossom, with blue flashing lights and Gregory Peck kneeling over me.

I said to him, '*Twelve O'Clock High*. I loved you in that.'

I don't remember anything after that.

ESTATE IN SHOCK

All was quiet today on the Fruit Bowl Estate as residents tried to come to terms with the tragedy of Tuesday's riot. A haze still hangs over the estate, and the blackened concrete and cracked windows are a terrible reminder of the events that have shocked the nation.

The night of violence followed a day of unrest, after 5-year-old Jade Bing was injured during a police operation.

At a press conference earlier on Tuesday, Deputy Assistant Commissioner Ray Stafford denied allegations that unnecessary force had been used. He refused to answer questions concerning the whereabouts of Jade's mother, believed to be in custody, or to discuss whether she would be allowed to visit her daughter in hospital.

Protesters then returned to the estate, and as their anger boiled over, police reinforcements were brought in, but failed to prevent widespread arson and looting.

Several arrests were made at the scene, and it is believed that some under-16s may be helping the police with their inquiries, but there have been no further statements since the announcement this morning that there will be an official investigation into the death of PC Ian Smalley.

Along the scorched walkways today, people gathered in small groups, stunned by the horror that erupted in their midst. PC Smalley was a familiar face on the estate.

Pensioner Olive Rankin said, 'I thought it was fireworks at first. I've been asking for a transfer out of here for years. I've been burgled five times and I've had to have a new hip. It's a terrible thing about the constable, though. It's his wife and kiddies I feel sorry for.'

Standing in front of the burned-out shell of his general store, Kareem Abbas said, 'I'm finished with this place.'

PC Smalley's widow made an emotional plea for calm. She said, 'Ian lived for his work.' She also paid tribute to the courage of Miss Birdie Gibbs, the pensioner who tried to rescue the young constable from the blaze. Miss Gibbs suffered minor burns and smoke inhalation, but is making a good recovery. *See story page 3.*

HAVE-A-GO HEROINE

The Apple Bough pensioner who braved the flames of Kareem's Kabin on Tuesday night in a bid to rescue PC Ian Smalley has been named as Birdie Gibbs. Mrs Gibbs, who is recovering in hospital, entered the blazing building and dragged Mr Smalley to a place of safety. Sadly, attempts to resuscitate the police officer were not successful and he was certified dead at the scene.

We can now reveal exclusively that this isn't the first time Plaistow-born Miss Gibbs has been commended for her bravery. Born Dora May Gibbs, in 1920, she volunteered for the London Fire Service at the outbreak of war.

Stationed at West Ham, she was selected for training as a despatch rider, in spite of being only five feet tall. She was awarded the George Medal for an act of gallantry during the blitzing of Beckton Gas Works.

Jen Marsh, an iridologist and detox

consultant, who is a close friend of Miss Gibbs said, 'She's just a totally brilliant person. I was down there. I saw what she did. It's all those years of Tory government that created this tragedy. Bad housing, Unemployment, Police brutality. It's just a totally bad scene here. Obviously, it's very sad about the man who died, but Birdie did her best. We're going to nominate her for a Golden Citizen Award.'

Croft Oak Burns Unit say Miss Gibbs is making an excellent recovery. They're appealing to the public not to phone with enquiries or get-well messages. They say their switchboard has been swamped, including calls from TV shows and national newspapers, eager to talk to the celebrity Gran.

Tragic Jade Waits For Mum. See full story pages 6 and 7.

Blanche brought him in to see me, and all he could say, over and over, was, 'I'm sorry, Mrs Gibbs, I'm sorry.'

They'd kept him in the remand wing at some young offenders place till Wilf and Blanche could get back. Scared the bejaysus out of him, and quite right too. They let him go with a caution, and I think it's all he needed. He'll be having nightmares for the rest of his life about that young copper. Fine young man like that, nice family man, gone to waste, and all for a bunch of thieving, sponging, brain-dead skivers, filling their pockets with cigs and Special Brew and a few bottles of the hard stuff. That's all they'd got on them when they found them, flaked out round the back. And Clark, of course, with all those choco-late bars melting on him.

Blanche said he swore to her he only went to see what everybody was doing in there. She says he never really meant to take anything. Jumped up into his arms, they did. Bounty bars do that if you don't watch them.

He just stood there hanging his head. Wouldn't look at me. Just as well. I'd got no eyebrows left, and not much hair on the front, either.

I said, 'Some honeymoon, Blanche.'

'Not to worry,' she said. 'We probably would have come back early anyway. I never slept a wink with Wilf's snoring. And you should see the prices down there. One pound twenty for a pot of tea, and it was only teabags.'

It was hard to talk. It hurt when I moved my face, except just after they gave me an injection. Then everything felt lovely.

She said, 'I suppose you know you're in the paper? Great big spread. Wilf's cut it out and kept it for when you come home.'

I said, 'If I come home. I think I've just about had it with the Fruit Bowl.'

She said, 'Oh, don't say that, Birdie. It wouldn't be Apple Bough without you. You'll feel different, once you're back amongst your own bits and pieces. Get some fresh wallpaper up. Wilf'll do it. You'll see.'

But I really didn't think I would. With Kareem's Kabin gone, and Clarice in Lime Trees, waiting to roll a seven, and Wilf spoken for. And they still haven't nailed Big Dwayne. Sitting in Spratt Hall lock-up he was, while the dirty deeds were being done, and as alibis go that's twenty-four-carat gold. That Janice'll be the one to take the fall this time. All that stuff they found in her flat – regular little home-worker she turned out to be.

I said, 'No, I shall ask for a transfer. On compassionate grounds. This could be my big chance. That Jen always said it was bad sheng fuey, and I think she was right, for once in her life.'

That started him off crying again.

I said, 'You can cut that out. You're supposed to be cheering me up. You're supposed to bring me a bottle of Lucozade and some nice fresh pyjamas. Sitting there using all my Kleenex.'

I gave him a little hug – best I could with all that stuff strapped along my arm. He's got to get over it, get back on the straight and narrow. Do something with his life. Do something good, for PC Smalley's sake. That's what I told him.

He was still sniffing. He said, 'I don't want you to leave.'

I said, 'Well, I'm going to, so you'd better start saving up for a push-bike.'

After they'd gone, the big black nurse came and gave me a wipe-down and a nice shot. 'Anything you want?' she said.

214

I said, 'Yes. A seaview flat and a lifetime's supply of whatever that stuff is.' After one of those injections everything's pink marshmallows. You can doze off, if you want to, or just float there and have a little daydream. Walk all the way along the seafront with Vanessa and the Goofer, have a battered saveloy and a carton of peas, and finish up at the Richmond for a lovely cold draught Guinness. You can do anything. I'd just won Jitterbug Queen again at the Paramount when that nurse came and woke me up.

She said, 'I shouldn't really let you have any more visitors today, but if I send this one away I don't think his bouquet'll last the night.'

He was a sight for sore eyes. Lovely sheepskin overcoat, nice white shirt, green tie and a great big bunch of irises. They were all right. They are a flower that does go off very quickly.

He was shaken, I could tell, when he saw the state I was in. Great red forehead on me and no eyelashes. Blew me a kiss, though, just like old times. Cologne, I could smell on him, too. Cologne, Brylcreem and dogs.

'Hello, Bird,' he said, 'I've had a bit of luck.'

Here I go again. I hear those trumpets blow again. I'm aglow again. Taking a chance on love.